love

is both

wave

and

particle

love

is both

wave

and

particle

Paul Cody

ROARING BROOK PRESS
New York

Text copyright © 2017 by Paul Cody
Published by Roaring Brook Press
Roaring Brook Press is a division of Holtzbrinck Publishing
Holdings Limited Partnership
175 Fifth Avenue, New York, NY 10010

fiercereads.com

Library of Congress Cataloging-in-Publication Data

Names: Cody, Paul, 1953– author.
Title: Love is both wave and particle / Paul Cody.
Description: First edition. | New York : Roaring Brook Press, 2017. |
    Summary: In this love story set in Ithaca, New York, at an alternative
    high school whose two requirements for admission are academic excellence
    and psychiatric disability, a boy and girl work on their yearlong senior
    project to write their life stories as informed by the points of view of
    people who have known them through their lives.
Identifiers: LCCN 2016038469 (print) | LCCN 2017008529 (ebook) | ISBN
    9781626726888 (hardback) | ISBN 9781626726871 (ebook)
Subjects: | CYAC: Love—Fiction. | Dating (Social customs)—Fiction. |
    Identity—Fiction. | Gifted children—Fiction. | Mental illness—Fiction.
    | Alternative schools—Fiction. | Schools—Fiction. | Ithaca
    (N.Y.)—Fiction. | BISAC: JUVENILE FICTION / Social Issues / Dating & Sex.
    | JUVENILE FICTION / Social Issues / Depression & Mental Illness. |
    JUVENILE FICTION / Family / Parents.
Classification: LCC PZ7.1.C633 Lo 2017 (print) | LCC PZ7.1.C633 (ebook) | DDC
    [Fic]—dc23
LC record available at https://lccn.loc.gov/2016038469

Our books may be purchased in bulk for promotional, educational, or business use.
Please contact your local bookseller or the Macmillan Corporate and Premium
Sales Department at (800) 221-7945 ext. 5442 or by e-mail at
MacmillanSpecialMarkets@macmillan.com.

First edition 2017
Book design by Elizabeth H. Clark
Printed in the United States of America

1   3   5   7   9   10   8   6   4   2

For Faye Bender

It seems as though we must use sometimes the one theory and sometimes the other, while at times we may use either. We are faced with a new kind of difficulty. We have two contradictory pictures of reality; separately neither of them fully explains the phenomena of light, but together they do.

—ALBERT EINSTEIN

I scarcely dared to look
To see what it was I was.

—ELIZABETH BISHOP,
"In the Waiting Room"

One

~~~~~~

Levon

The fat lady across the street died. At home, on Sunday.
The one in the green house with the aluminum siding.
Susan, my mom, told me in an email. She saw it in the local
paper, the *Ithaca Journal*, at work, on Tuesday.

At first Susan wasn't sure if it was the thin woman or
the fat woman. There was also a really short fat guy who
lived there. You hardly ever saw any of them. The shades
were always drawn, and they never used the front door.
Except every once in a while an ambulance would pull up
at night and they'd take the fat guy out on a stretcher, with
an oxygen mask on his face.

If anything, we thought he'd be the first to go. They
all seemed to be in their sixties or seventies, and they never
seemed to go out except to get in this gray Chevrolet Im-
pala, maybe to go grocery shopping or to the doctor. Once
in a while one of the women would come out to the front

porch to get the mail. Or the skinny woman or the fat woman would take the trash out to the strip of grass between the sidewalk and street, where the city had planted trees, on the side street from the back, because their house was on the corner.

Sometimes, if you passed them and they happened to be on the porch or taking the trash out or getting in the car, they'd nod or say hello, and I'd nod or say hello back. You never saw anybody visit, anybody stop in to have a cup of coffee or a beer or whatever people do when they visit each other. That was it. In fifteen or twenty years.

Well, seventeen years, because that's how old I was. But Susan was forty-three, and we'd lived across the street from them for all that time. And I don't think I ever said a word to the fat man, because I almost never saw him except when the ambulance was taking him away—always at night, and always out the front door on a stretcher, down the steps, the red light on top flashing and twirling, and the oxygen mask on his face. And I'd think, Maybe this is his last ride.

A few times I saw him standing in the driveway at the back of the house, on the side street, wearing a white shirt and dark pants, looking very neat, but strange because he was one of those people who was pretty much as wide as he was tall. He had a square face and black hair that was neatly combed back off his forehead.

The fat woman was not that wide, and had a round face and reddish hair, and none of them looked like each other, and Susan said none of them, as far as she knew, were related.

The fat lady who died was Dakota Goddell, the man was Harold W. Smithie, and the thin woman was Martha Nelson.

The name Dakota surprised me. She looked like a Mary or an Alice or a Kathy or a Norma. The obituary in the *Journal* said she was sixty-two, had died at home after a brief illness, and had "enjoyed living in the country and worked on farms prior to relocating to Ithaca in 1986. She loved animals and had owned many dogs. Dakota was a friendly person who never disagreed with anyone. She was always happy and never shirked a task. Survivors include friends and companions Harold W. Smithie and Martha Nelson." That was all.

I tried to remember what I had been doing Sunday night. I'm sure I was home because I don't go out much. They must have called the police or an ambulance or something to take the body away, but I didn't notice, didn't know, didn't have any idea that the fat lady, that Dakota Goddell, who had lived across the street for so many years, had died.

And so often over the years, four or five or six times, I had watched from the curtains at the front door as they took

Mr. Smithie down the steps on a stretcher, with an oxygen mask on his face, and every time I had thought, This is it. He won't be back. This is the last time.

I always thought of the closed curtains, and what life must be like for them, and where they came from, and what they did all day.

And that's how this whole thing began—with Meg, my teacher, counselor, adviser, shrink at this special school I went to, who said I had to write a senior project to graduate. And how I met Sam, who was new to the town and the school, and had just spent most of a year in mental hospitals.

This was an English/writing seminar. We were to write a few pages each week about our lives, past and present. What we were doing and thinking, what our pasts had been like. We'd spend all of senior year on this. I would show nobody what I wrote except for Meg and Sam. Sam and I would read each other's versions and make comments and suggestions. The idea was to come to a deeper understanding of both ourselves and our pasts. And Meg would contact other people for us to solicit stories about us, and other students' versions of senior year, but she would limit telling anyone about the specifics or scope of the project, and they would be sworn to secrecy. She'd talk to former teachers, shrinks, roommates, fellow students, parents, anyone whose name she could come up with from our files. Meg would withhold outside input from us till the end of the year. The whole thing was pretty funny because I'd never met Samantha, who preferred to be called Sam. Just heard a little about her from Meg.

We were both supposed to be gifted, and we were both on meds, and we were both avoidant, or maybe somewhere on the broad spectrum of Asperger's, or depressed or ADD or something else the psychiatrists pulled out of the DSM-5, the *Diagnostic and Statistical Manual of Mental Disorders*. Because everything needs a label, right? Everything fits into a neat little box? Then we can understand it and treat it, usually with drugs? Especially human beings? Their histories and souls?

Not that Meg did that, or even Susan, who was a neurobiologist. It was just kind of the way things went. When the boxes they put us in spilled over and fell off the shelves, everybody—honest to God—meant well, and they didn't want anyone, especially us kids, to get hurt. But it was really just about taking a complex kid, struggling to grow up, and giving him some labels so you had a set of symptoms you could treat and have a more orderly classroom. All of it was made up in the end.

I wouldn't even have considered doing the project, but I'd known Meg a long time, for all five years I'd been at the school, and I trusted her as much as I trusted anybody, maybe even my mom. And she said that she thought that Sam was talented, really talented, and complicated, and vulnerable. Sam was reluctant but willing.

This would be a yearlong project, Meg said. Who knew? she said. It could be a book people might read someday.

Meg said, I told her you were one of the most interesting kids in the school. And by far the best-read.

She smiled. And I said you were a nice guy, and occasionally charming.

I said, Oh.

And between you and me, kiddo, she's one of the most interesting, brightest kids I've come across in ages. Extremely well-read. And potentially funny and charming, if—if you can draw her out.

She handed me a piece of paper that had the name Sam and her email address.

She has yours, Meg said, but I think you make the first play. Otherwise I doubt you'll hear from her.

The paper was a pink Post-it note with the name Sam printed clearly, and the initials sav, three numerals, a star, a pound sign, two parenthesis signs with a question mark between the parens, @gmail.com.

I'd never seen such a strange email address.

This is her email? I asked Meg.

Exactly, she said.

Two

Sam

So I got an email from this dude named Levon. Meg from the Clock School warned me about it. Said we were gonna do this senior project together. Well, not together exactly, but at the same time. Parallel projects writing our own autobiographies. It was English and writing, with maybe some psychology and personal history thrown in. He'd do his, I'd do mine, and we'd show each other what we were doing as we went along. Give each other feedback and such. Make suggestions. Advise and encourage.

Meg didn't exactly say where she'd come into the picture. If we would be meeting with her too, and with each other. Me and Levon. Pronounced LEE-von.

School didn't start officially for a week, even though things at the Clock School seemed pretty loose. They sort of have classes but they sort of don't. They have a lot of teachers and staff, and a lot of rooms with couches and easy chairs, and labs with computers, and a big room where kids build robots.

The school was on the second floor of this big old factory building where they used to make the Ithaca Calendar Clock, which was supposedly famous in the nineteenth century. Now it was completely overhauled. There was a music store on the first floor, and music teachers, and some offices for shrinks, and a massage therapist and a yoga studio. It was all very Ithaca. And it was in this normal, kind of leafy neighborhood called Fall Creek, where the houses were kind of close together, and the houses were set close to the street, but had cool backyards, and apparently a lot of writers and professors and musicians and artists lived in Fall Creek.

The school was a charter school, grades seven to twelve, but you had to be diagnosed with something from the DSM to go there, and you also had to be pretty good at school and want very small classes where you got a lot of teacher attention and support. Most of the students were faculty brats from Cornell or Ithaca College, and they just didn't fit in very well anywhere else. The school got state and federal money, and the staff and parents wrote and got grants, and the Clock School was ridiculously well funded.

I got this info from my parents, Nathan and Vera.

Anyway, back to Levon, which, by the way, was a curious name. Like he came from Arkansas, or the Old Testament. And had a long beard and wore suspenders. He sounded possibly okay, like we might do this thing by email.

When I met Meg, she showed me around the school, and we sat in her office, and she was wearing shorts and flip-flops and was carrying a few extra pounds, but she was wearing this nice lavender top, and a silver necklace with a red stone. She showed me around the mostly empty school, then to her office, which was down a long hall, then went right on the short part of an L.

It was somehow on the inside of the L, so there were no windows, just exposed red brick and beams, but shiny oak floors. There was a wall mostly of books, and a small desk in a corner, but it was big and more like a den. There was a couch, a coffee table, two big comfortable chairs, and everything looked clean and used.

And I loved the art on the walls. Two Paul Klees—*Fish Magic* and the ship with the red and yellow flags—plus a big copy of John Singer Sargent's *The Daughters of Edward Darley Boit*, which has always struck me as incomparably beautiful and incredibly sad—each of the four daughters, from the toddler in the foreground in full light to the other three, recede into the background, then into darkness and obscurity as they go further into adolescence, framed by a large doorway and these gorgeous, tall, shapely vases, and nothing behind them but blackness.

I felt safe somehow in this room. In Meg's room. Maybe she got it about the Sargent painting.

So Levon. His email. He said, Hey Sam. He told me he had talked to Meg, and that while he wasn't wildly enthusiastic, he had to graduate, and he thought Meg was good people, the best. A very cool woman, in fact. He said he didn't mind how we did this. Text, Skype, email, phone, though he was not a big fan of the phone. He wasn't sure what Meg had in mind. The drill, the protocol. But he figured we could figure it out to our mutual satisfaction. Mutual satisfaction. He actually said that. Like a Henry James novel or something. Well, there it is. Well, where *what* is? *It* kept changing. And *where* was never quite clear. And *is* was shifting too. Beautifully ambiguous.

He said, Welcome to Ithaca. This is a pretty cool town. There's a lot of interesting stuff here for such a small place. Then he pastes in this thing he wrote about a fat lady who lived across the street who he barely knew and who had just died.

It was kind of interesting, but I didn't know what to make of it. It was sad, a little anyway. I mean, the woman's life sounded sad, and that she lived there so long and he hardly knew her was sad, and her obituary was sad. She liked dogs, never shirked a task, was always happy, never argued with anyone. Never? Anyone?

What struck me most of all was that he said he, Levon, never went out much, and in the last paragraph he wrote, I always thought of the closed curtains, and what life must be like for them, and where they came from, and what they did all day.

It was slightly creepy the way he watched them carry Mr. Smithie out on the stretcher so many times and thought he was going to die. And then Dakota Goddell died, and he didn't even know.

But it bothered him that he didn't know them, that she was gone, and he wondered about their lives. Not so much like being nosy or being a spy, but feeling curious and kind of feeling sorry for them.

And maybe too—and I wonder about this, I wonder if he was aware of this—he saw a little of himself in their lives. This guy behind closed curtains who didn't go out much. Who peeked out, and like Dakota, he had a slightly weird name.

I would never say this to him.

After the four pages, he wrote, This is what I have for now. I don't know if it means anything. But I hope to hear from you, and I'm looking forward.

I thought about it for a while. I sat on my bed on the third floor, and looked at the empty walls, which were empty because this had only been my room for like two months.

Finally, I wrote: Good. Okay.

Then I wrote down this poem I'd once made out of refrigerator magnets:

lick smooth
my shadow
together
whisper
weak music
say here her
feet rose
languid through
white summer

That's all for now, I wrote. There it is, as it were.

Fair skies and following seas.

I hit send.

A sailor's term for good luck. I wondered if he'd get that.

Three

Meg

I gathered they emailed each other. They didn't say anything about what they said, of course, but the first big hurdle was crossed. He wrote to her and she wrote back, and they both let me know. So that's a good thing.

But get this: they both expected this project was going to happen over email. Ha! They'd work together on a project over an entire school year, and they'd never have to lay eyes on each other. They'd never even have to be in the same room together at the same time.

I disabused them both of that idea immediately. I told them the three of us would be meeting Wednesday at ten o'clock, in my office, the first week of classes.

You can both wear masks and disguises, if you wish, but you will both be here, I said in my most imperative Meg Goldman voice.

I didn't hear back from either of them after that one, but

I was confident they'd be here. Sometimes kids like a lack of ambiguity.

I'd been working with kids, my Lord, almost twenty years. I got an undergraduate degree in English with the idea of being a teacher, and then after getting certified, I went on and got a master's in social work as well. I figured I'd be employable one way or the other. I did all of that at Syracuse, and then came down to Ithaca, which was like paradise.

Most people don't know it, but Syracuse is officially the snowiest city in the continental United States. It gets more snow than Buffalo, Fargo, Minneapolis, than anywhere. It has something to do with its proximity to Lake Erie, and air currents, so the winter is long and grim, and the city is not Paris. It's not even Cairo.

Ithaca has long, tough winters, but Ithaca is cool in so many ways I can't name them all. It has a major research university, a major college with a fine music conservatory. It has a wonderful unspoiled lake, a farmer's market, gorges, and really interesting people. Nabokov wrote most of *Lolita* here, and a significant part of its Ivy League institution is a state agricultural school, so people have cow shit on their shoes, and somehow, that keeps people, many of them anyway, just a little bit grounded.

I loved the town wholly and forever when I got here and started teaching English at Boynton Middle School.

I taught for four years, and the biggest surprise was how widely diverse the students were. There were plenty of university brats, but there were kids from the projects, and kids bussed in from the Town of (rather than the City of) Ithaca. I started learning about all the kids with special needs, and assessments, and IEPs, which stands for individualized education programs. It sounds weirdly close to IED, an improvised explosive device, used so widely in the Middle East.

IEPs were mandated by the state. What it meant was that if a kid was having trouble in school—couldn't keep up with schoolwork, was disruptive, couldn't sit still, was withdrawn, overly aggressive, anything that consistently stood out—the teacher would talk to the school social worker, the parent or parents would be brought in, and an assessment would be done. A special-ed person, a social worker, a teacher, and often an administrator would go over the kid's records at length, talk to the child's present and former teachers, and decide if this kid needed to be deemed a student with special needs. If the child was so deemed, then an IEP was drawn up by a team consisting of a psychologist, social worker, special-ed expert, and the child's teacher. It required that the child consult a doctor or psychiatrist. Meds were often dispensed.

The child might get counseling, a one-on-one aide in the classroom, hours out of the classroom being tutored, particular protocols of therapy, and physical or psychological or anger management therapy.

Essentially, our wealthy school system brought its considerable resources to help the child.

Basically, after four years of teaching English at Boynton, of watching IEP plans try to make up for messed-up homes and the quirks of biology and bad or overwhelmed parents, I was offered a job at the high school as a social worker. I thought, Now I can do some real work. Get in there with the kids and their families, and really get my hands bloody with dirt and grime and broken calluses. Plus no more papers to grade.

But boy, it was a ride. Five years in the dark heart of really broken families, of seriously damaged kids. One-parent families, or no-parent families, or parents addicted or alcoholic or in jail or on parole or under the supervision of the court. Sometimes the saddest cases were the kids living out in the trailer parks, a few living in the woods in abandoned buses, the incest, the sisters or half brothers or "aunts" or "cousins" trying to raise a whole brood of kids.

So many of them were listless; they had no light in their eyes. You could just look at them, and they were unwashed, and badly fed, and unloved. Many of them had parents who worked at Walmart or Burger King, or cleaned houses or hotel rooms, and still had to get food stamps.

The worst was when fourteen- or fifteen- or sixteen-year-old girls came in and told you they were pregnant and wanted so much to keep the baby. They were so happy. They would finally have something all their own.

This was by no means the majority of the students. Many of the I-High kids were worrying about getting into Princeton or Williams, or whether they should take a gap year. They had, as we say, first world problems.

But after five years, I started to feel bleak. I'd come home after work with this feeling of heaviness, with something like despair.

Then I started hearing about the Clock School. Special needs, but kids who were generally quite good students, but wanted really small classes and lots of attention. A charter school for grades seven to twelve. State, city, and federal funds, plus grant money. They were talking about roughly 150 students, twenty-five per grade. A staff-to-student ratio of one to five, which was outrageous, and few of those staff would be administrators.

It took over two years to get it off the ground, to get it funded, to get the Calendar Clock Building renovated, to hire staff, but, man, boy oh boy, I wanted it. One of the big arguments for it was that some gifted kids were so bored in regular classes, even in Advanced Placement classes, that they just checked out. They basically said, Fuck this. They became disruptive, depressed, disengaged.

So I applied for and got the job at the Clock School. And the kids there were amazing.

I remember first reading Levon's file and seeing that in the fourth grade he was tested in reading, and he was at the level of someone in the third month of the twelfth grade. It was so at odds with his class performance that they retested him, and he tested at the sixth month of the twelfth grade. In science he tested below grade level, despite the fact that his mother taught neurobiology at Cornell. *WTF?* his teachers seemed to think, but didn't the fact that there was no father on the scene, ever, have something to do with it?

Or that Sam, whose file is thick as a Dickens novel, consistently tested in the mid- to high 130s in both Stanford-Binet and Wechsler intelligence tests, and always underperformed in school. Because of something in the DSM? Because she took more than a dozen different meds between the ages of seven and sixteen? Because she cut? Didn't get out of bed for days? Had nearly a dozen rounds of electroconvulsive therapy at age sixteen?

I knew that her father, Nathan, had worked seventy hours a week as a vice president at Fidelity in Boston, as the top IT specialist in computer security, which is to say that he was chief guard for nearly one or two trillion dollars in investments, virtually all of which traveled by computer, but he gave that up for the less stressful position of guarding Harvard's thirty billion dollars in investments, and now guards Cornell's modest six-billion-dollar portfolio.

And that her mother, Vera, a trained economist, according to the file, seems never to have worked since her only child was born, but has poured her considerable intelligence and energy into anxiously hovering over her daughter, making sure she was all right, then just ignoring her. Which is to say, according to one postdoc at McLean, the famous psychiatric hospital associated with Harvard Medical School, making sure she was sick. After last fall at McLean, Nathan and Vera left Chestnut Hill and Boston, came to Ithaca, and Sam spent the spring semester, as it were, at Austen Riggs, a topflight treatment center for the very rich in the Berkshires, which is closer to Ithaca.

She graduated, as though from school, in May.

Meanwhile, I do not have a partner, since Rob and I split two years ago.

I am forty-three years old, and I have a wonderful chocolate Lab named Buster. We walk in the woods on the Finger Lakes Trails. In the fall, when it's cool in the shade of the woods, and Buster has raced ahead of me, I'll rest, my back against a tree, in an open spot, my face to the warm sun. I'll close my eyes, and hear Buster's feet pounding toward me. He'll lick my face, scratch my shoulder with his paw as if to say, C'mon. Let's go. Stop sitting.

I'll think, This is good.

I forget for the moment that most kids in the world, that many in this affluent, sweet city, have very little of what is good in life. That even the kids who seem to have everything are often as broken and lonely as dolls, naked, missing limbs and eyes, discarded in woods, next to rest stops, just off the tens of thousands of miles of interstates of our country.

Four

~~~~~~~

Chloe

*There were no single rooms at McLean, not in the adoles-*cent units anyway, and that was because they didn't want any of us to "isolate," to be cut off from the world and other people. It was part of the "therapeutic" and "socialization" process. That's what they called it anyway.

So it was me and Sam, pretty much the whole time I was there, which was from September, last year, to December. Then I was an outpatient, going to appointments three times a week, and then by this summer they got my meds settled, which is to say, they got me settled. And so it's back to Miss Porter's School in another week for me, just about. So no more cutting, no more bingeing and purging, no more crazy shit. No more McLean.

Just a nice pretty rich girl going to a rich girl's school, then maybe a pretty good college, if I can get into one. The McLean stay kind of put a wrinkle in the works. I took my junior year off to be crazy. Do I write that in my application to Smith or Wellesley or Bard? Probably, most likely, I'll spend an extra year at Miss Porter's.

I got there about a week after Sam did. I think the first week of September. Instead of boarding school, our family SUV pulled up at the reception area at McLean in the morning, and they unloaded me and my baggage (hahahaha), and there's a lot of baggage in every way. At that point, to be honest, I didn't give a shit. I was so fucking tired. I so didn't care about anything anymore. They could have dumped my useless carcass in a field somewhere, or on the bank of some weedy river or marsh, and I would have curled up and stayed there forever.

After about five interviews and three days in the medical unit, they brought me to the room I was gonna share with Sam, and she wasn't there. The only thing I noticed was how neat everything was. Clothes hung in her closet, a few pair of shoes, some Birks and Docs, a bunch of books lined up on the shelves over her desk, and her bed really neatly and tightly made.

I thought, How does anybody have the energy to be neat and organized? How can anyone care that much about shit like that?

And it was funny because at that moment she was having the first of her ECT treatments, which I found out about later, when they wheeled her down the hallway in a wheelchair, and she was not with it. She was under it. From the sedatives and the volts of electricity to her brain, from being so depressed she could hardly move her hands even.

When she came to the room a few hours later, the two nurses, or aides, got her out of the chair and into the bed, and she was wearing yoga pants and a loose top, and a nice black V-neck sweater. Her left wrist had a big white bandage around it. They got the pillows under her head, the covers over her, then they took the hairnet off, and she had great hair. Brownish-blond, and a little frizzy, like one of those Botticellis in art history class. It looked soft and beautiful, and you wanted to stroke it to see if it was as soft as it looked.

The nurse said that this was Sam, my roommate, and that she'd need to sleep awhile, and I said that was good with me.

I didn't know at the time she'd just been shocked, but she looked pretty messed up and vulnerable, like a sleeping, damaged princess, and I felt something new and funny. I felt kind of sorry for her. And somehow, that didn't feel right. It felt like it did matter.

She started to stir around eleven, to move her arms and head, and then a nurse came in with a tray of crackers and juice. I had been quietly unpacking my junk, clothes and shoes, a few books, stuff for the bathroom, and I was sitting up on my bed, looking through the folders they gave you when they released you to the less restrictive wards. Rules and Regulations, Your Safety, Treatment Modalities, and a social worker had come in somewhere along there to say hello. She was Kim, and she looked too young and too cute to be a social worker, and she said lunch would be at twelve thirty, and an aide would come by to show me where to go, and she asked me if I was getting settled okay, and I said, Sure.

Lemme know if you need anything? She patted my shoulder and I thought, I need a new life, a new attitude, a new everything, but I didn't say any of that at the time. I'd promised my mom that I'd do my best, that I'd at least try to get with the program, whatever the program was.

The nurse put the tray down next to Sam's bed, and shook her arm a little, and Sam made noises, and the nurse said, Sam, time to get up. The sun's out.

And I noticed it was. It was streaming through the big windows, it was shining in the leaves of the trees outside.

Sam opened her eyes, and they were brown, and set far apart, and she blinked, and tried to sit up but couldn't at first. But the nurse got her sitting up in the bed, put a few pillows behind her back, poured some juice for her, opened a small package of crackers, and Sam sat there with her head on her chest.

Okay, Sam, the nurse said, we've gotta get some food in you.

Sam blinked some more, and she turned and looked at me, and she said, almost in a whisper, Hey, you're Chloe, then she closed her eyes again.

That's Chloe, the nurse said, your roommate, and I said, Hey.

And it was funny, but I was moved that she knew my name, and that the first thing she said after coming out of the fog was to acknowledge my existence.

I watched her sip orange juice and bite the corner of a cracker.

Good, the nurse said.

Yummy, Sam said, and the nurse laughed.

The nurse took her blood pressure and checked her pulse, and again said, Good. Then she said she was going to check on someone down the hall, and asked me if I could keep an eye on Sam.

Just don't have her up walking around yet, the nurse said.

I said, Sure.

Then we were alone, and Sam said, ECT. Electroconvulsive therapy. Shock therapy.

I nodded, but I was kind of shocked.

How was that? I asked after a while.

Kind of fuzzy, she said. They drug the shit out of you first, so I don't remember much. But I don't know if it's the drugs or the ECT. The tee hee hee.

So that was how I first met Sam, and until she left, the week before Christmas, we were together pretty much all the time. I mean, not all the time. But a ton.

The first three weeks, she was getting ECT twice a week, and I don't know what she was like before, but she was definitely not paralyzed with depression after that. She was fuzzy and funny and pretty forgetful, but she was up and moving slowly around. I pictured bolts of lightning in the dark sky of her brain.

We walked around outside with an aide, and she spent a fair bit of time reading. In the lounge, which had big couches and chairs, and in quiet rooms, where you could read or use your computer or write in a journal or write letters.

It was kind of like Miss Porter's, in some ways. Rich girls, only here, oddly, ironically, they were better behaved. Maybe because of the drugs, or the fact that there were way fewer of us. On our unit, there were just twelve of us, and my God, there was enough staff for fifty. Doctors and interns, nurses, aides, social workers, recreational and physical therapists, psychologists, grad students in biology, neurology, psychology, social work, public health. I don't know what else.

I'm from Philadelphia, Mount Airy, much of which is pretty ritzy. And Sam is from Chestnut Hill, which is just outside of Boston, like McLean, and very ritzy. We didn't talk a lot during those first three or four weeks, when she was getting zapped. There were two other ECT girls on our unit—Melanie, who was pretty overweight, and way depressed, and Lila, who was small and had long black hair that usually covered her face. Lila was always cold, so she wore a ski sweater and one of those Peruvian hats with the earflaps and the strings hanging down from the earflaps.

Maybe they were getting more voltage than Sam, or more sessions a week, but they seemed way more out of it. Not that Sam wasn't fuzzy and foggy and forgetful, but she was up and around and doing things. She told me a little about herself. That she had no sisters or brothers, that her dad used to work for Fidelity, and now worked for Harvard in finance and IT security, and that they were probably moving to Ithaca in New York so he could work for Cornell. He was tired of working sixty- and seventy-hour weeks. Her mom used to be a banker in New York City before Sam was born, but after Sam was born, Sam was her full-time job.

I was one of seven kids. Catholics, I told her. The middle of seven, and I was the designated fuck-up. Both my parents were attorneys, were partners in law firms in Philly. We probably had opposite problems. I got no attention; she got way too much.

But there was something about Sam. She was just so

gracious and thoughtful and kind. I felt like such a piece of shit, and she treated me like I was someone special, like I was someone with dignity, and deserved respect, and it started to kind of rub off on me. That if someone like this could think so well of me, and treat me so well and thoughtfully, then maybe I could treat myself that way too. Like just being with Sam made me respect myself more.

Even though she was one of the ECT girls and wasn't required to do much, like go to group, gym, or any of the therapy stuff except individual, she was usually in one of the quiet rooms, the lounges, in a big chair, under a blanket, reading. And she didn't read crap. She was reading *Lord Jim* and Henry James and Willa Cather, and the thing that impressed the hell out of me, she was reading James Joyce. When I said something about that, she said, Oh, it's only *A Portrait*. That's like climbing Mount Washington. *Ulysses* is K2. Then she started to tell me about this German book, *The Magic Mountain*, where all these people are stuck for years in a TB sanitarium in the Alps.

Kind of like here, I said, and she laughed.

Except a bunch of them die, and it ends in World War I, and that sucks.

By the end of September, I think, her ECT sessions were done. They'd switched up meds on both of us, and neither of us could sleep. We'd lie in the dark and talk, and it was almost like we were little kids. I told her about going in our giant Suburban to our lake house in the Poconos, and how at night we built campfires and toasted marshmallows, and tried to tell ghost stories, but they only scared my youngest brother, Tad. And how going to bed really late on the sleeping porch there was a wonderful smell of wood smoke and lake and pine trees and wet towels and bathing suits. There was the sound of crickets, and moonlight, and it was delicious to lie there, so, so tired, but not wanting to sleep yet.

Sam was quiet for a while.

That sounds gorgeous, she finally said.

You know what I could go for right now? I said.

Yeah?

A cigarette.

You think we could bum one from Juanita? Sam asked, which surprised me.

Juanita was a grad student who sometimes worked the night shift. We knew she smoked because we'd hear her prop the door open onto the patio, and we could smell the smoke.

Sam called her Wan. She said, Why so pale and wan, fond lover? Why so pale and wan? It was from some old poem.

We went out to the lounge, and the office next to the lounge.

Wan was staring at her computer.

Wan, I said, we can't sleep, and we were wondering, I began.

We're dying for a smoke, Sam said.

Wan said, You girls.

You could tell Wan really liked and trusted Sam.

Just one, Sam said.

Wan smiled. Don't breathe a word. And stay on the patio.

She took a pack of Newport 100s from her bag, gave us each one, and said, Use the doorstop to prop the door open.

We were leaving the office, and she said, Girls.

We turned, and she was holding up a yellow lighter.

Outside was beautiful, and though the moon wasn't full, it was pretty close. One of those big October moons.

We sat on the patio steps, under a big oak tree that had dark scarlet leaves. We lit our cigs, and Sam coughed, and then we just sat and looked out. It must have been two or three in the morning, and it's something I remember most of all. Because the cigarettes tasted so good, and we didn't say anything. Just the two of us, like old soldiers, understanding something we couldn't say.

Five

~~~~~~

Sam

Classes at the Clock School started the Tuesday after Labor Day, and it was kind of funny because the last official school I'd gone to was Groton, which was as WASP-y as it gets, and tony as all get-out, with quads and old red brick, and oak trees that went back to the Civil War, or to Roosevelt's time, and you never knew which Roosevelt—Franklin or Teddy—though I'm not sure if both of them went there. Now I was going to school in an old factory building, which was whitewashed, but you could still see the black lettering under the paint—Ithaca Calendar Clock. I kind of liked it, because I had hated Groton, just as I read somewhere that Roosevelt—I think FDR—had hated Groton. Good for him.

I'd been to the Clock School twice, in midsummer with my mom and dad, and then later to meet with Meg. The summer in Ithaca had gone well, not that I'd done much.

Dad was around much more; none of those Fidelity days when a car picked him up at seven in the morning and often dropped him off at nine or ten at night. He'd also ditched the black Benz for an Accord, and Mom gave up her Lexus for an Austin Mini. A red Mini, but still. Dad worked more or less normal hours, and he taught me to drive, first in the high school parking lot, then in this beautiful park that had small roads that ran along the southern end of Cayuga Lake, which is one of those giant Finger Lakes that are thirty or forty miles long. Then in a cemetery that had a view of the lake, then along the roads in Cayuga Heights, which is the fancy neighborhood in Ithaca.

By Chestnut Hill standards, it was modest. No ten-thousand-square-foot houses. You could see the houses from the road, and our house, which was relatively big, but not crazy big, had been owned by a retired horticulture professor, and the yard was unbelievably beautiful. I mean, all kinds of trees and plants and small terraces, all on a small scale, but it was like you could die there happy.

I had two rooms to myself on the third floor, with slanted ceilings, a couch, two big chairs, my desk, bed, bookcases, and these great old leaded windows. I had my own bathroom. It felt good up there. It felt like home.

By July, I had my license, and Dad bought me an orange Honda Fit.

I didn't know anyone, but the town was small enough,

and I was on lithium and a small dose of lorazepam for anxiety, so I felt pretty comfortable driving around, parking near downtown, getting coffee at this place called Gimme!, then sitting in a park shaped like a triangle, which was next to a brook. The town felt mellow and right-sized. It felt like a place I could reason with.

By late August it started to get noticeably busier. You'd see a lot of rental trucks and vans, and stupid me, it took me two days to realize that the college students were coming back. Between Cornell and Ithaca College, twenty-five thousand college students were moving back. You could feel the energy, and the streets were way more clogged with cars.

So Tuesday: eight fifty a.m. I parked on this leafy Fall Creek street. No problem with parking. All these neat, funky-looking houses. Buddhist prayer flags over some front doors, No Fracking Way signs on some front lawns, kind of like Cambridge.

I went in the side door of the big white building, and there was a table, and a man and woman, teacher-like, were handing out folders in the lobby. Upper-school, lower-school. I went to the upper-school guy, who had a beard and was wearing a suit coat over a T-shirt. Hello, he said. You look new.

I nodded.

He put his hand out and we shook.

And you are?

Sam Vash.

Yes, I've heard of you.

It kind of made me start. I felt myself blushing.

Shit, I thought. Shit. Shit. Should've taken an extra lorazepam.

Nothing but praise, he said. Chuck Vallely. English. But I'm afraid Meg's claimed you. I get to feed the robotics kids. Give them their sci-fi.

He nodded and smiled more.

Upstairs to the Big Room.

I took the folder, which had my name typed on a sticker in the upper right corner. Samantha Ariel Vash.

I went up the wide staircase, which was polished oak and had oak banisters. It was startling, the contrast between the inside and outside of the building. I was also startled by how little some of the kids were, how small and nervous they seemed. They must have been eleven, twelve years old. Was I them? I thought. Starting at the start?

They were thin and awkward, and they seemed to be trying hard to hug the walls, to stay low and unseen. But you could also see that they were trying hard to wear the right clothes, the canvas sneakers, the hair ties, the short skirt or the jeans with the huge rips in the knees.

At the top of the stairs was a long hallway they called Main Street, which was wide and carpeted. Everything else was windows, and refurbished brick, and old beams, and new oak supporting the beams.

We were directed to the Big Room, which was a small auditorium that sat maybe three hundred. It was beautifully done. They had somehow cut into the floor above, and it was tall and spacious, and the seats were inclined. Four people were sitting on the stage, and kids were clustering into groups. More or less by age and friendship. There were six or seven kids near the front, older kids, all wearing tie-dyed T-shirts, all but one with glasses, and I was betting ten to one that these were the robotics kids.

The kids looked more or less normal, though the kids at McLean and Austen Riggs had always seemed kind of normal, until you dug a little below the surface or spent time with them. They all had their stories, though. I guess everybody has their stories.

A big guy in a dark blue checked shirt got up first with a handheld microphone. He said, Okay, everybody, seats, please. Time for kickoff.

I was in the top row, on the side, on an aisle, and I could see everybody. While Gus, the principal, was saying, Welcome back, we're gonna have a great year, I was kind of scanning the room. I saw Meg down near the front, in an aisle seat, and I guess, without realizing it, I was looking for Levon.

I had no idea who I was looking for. A short chunky guy

with bad glasses, a medium skinny guy who twitched, someone with a ponytail or rat-tail, someone in tie-dye, but I guessed that was the science kids. There was a group you could tell were the art kids. They wore black, and had part of their hair shaved, and had tats and piercings. It was the same everywhere—at Groton, McLean, Austen Riggs.

Then a woman, a social worker, was saying that she was always available, she was here all the time, her door was always open, and then a kind of severe-looking woman with very short helmet hair and a suit, who was the nurse practitioner, said she was at the school Monday, Wednesday, and Friday afternoons, and she said her specialty was psychiatric meds, and her door was always open.

The last guy was big and shambly and kind of old, maybe in his sixties. He wore a baggy tweed jacket, a shirt with a button-down collar, and corduroy pants. He spoke softly. He was the school psychologist. His name was Ron and he just wanted to say one thing. He said, If you're trying to move a box, and it's not too big, then you can probably move it by yourself. No problem. But if you're trying to move a couch, you can't do it by yourself, no matter how big and strong you are. You need someone on the other end. So if the box is really heavy, and really uncomfortable, and is really painful to move, then it's probably a couch. That's when you need to get some help. That's when you talk to one of us. Any of us. It made sense. I liked this guy Ron.

Then we broke up and went to different classes, though they weren't like other classes I'd been to. One was called Quest for Justice, and there were five of us, plus Justine, the teacher. She was maybe fifty, had gray hair, and her glasses kept slipping down her nose. We talked about what we would read—Voltaire, Camus, Seneca, a little Plato and Nietzsche, some novels later in the year. There was the Biology of Ecology and there were three of us in there, and then art class, which had about ten of us in this big room, and the teacher was Francine, and I liked her. She wore a smock and black tights, and she said we could do what we wanted, but that she wanted us to try a little of everything. Clay, silk-screening, oils, watercolor, digital, which might be fun.

A guy named Andre, who was tall and had black hair and multiple piercings in both ears, was very friendly and kept showing me different things in the studio, then Francine called him over, and this girl who was short and really pretty and had warm eyes came over. She said, Hey, Sam, welcome. Just want to warn you—Andre thinks he's the biggest player in all of Ithaca, but he understands the word *no*.

We laughed, and she said, Wanna go outside for a break?

I said, Sure. I need air.

She said, Me too. I'm Anna.

We went down some stairs, through a heavy steel door,

and there was an old parking lot, and a beat-up picnic table with an old coffee can for butts. She took out ChapStick, did her lips, offered it to me. I passed.

You doing okay? she asked. First day?

Yeah, it's pretty loose, I said.

Yeah, it's chill. People do some pretty cool stuff. Interesting stuff.

We sat a little and picked at the worn wood of the table.

Who's your main teacher? she asked.

Meg.

The Megster, Anna said, and nodded.

She good?

Very good. And I heard she'll team you up with Levon.

Is that good?

She blinked and looked thoughtful. Finally she said, An extremely interesting boy. Could be a disaster, could be brilliant.

How do you mean?

She smiled, kind of mysteriously. I spent half of last year trying to sleep with Levon, she said. No luck. I know at least three other girls, all lookers, who've done the same thing. Same result. I'll say no more. You'll see.

We exchanged cell numbers and email addresses, and Anna became my first Ithaca friend.

I went back inside and things felt more relaxed, or I felt more relaxed. I hadn't realized that all day I'd had this first-day-of-school anxiety. I hadn't been in a *normal* school in over a year, and the last one had ended in disaster. I had this awful, deep fear that one wrong move, and I'd be back at McLean or Austen Riggs. This all felt, part of it, at least, like one huge trial. And I noticed that the younger kids, too, weren't hugging the walls so much, that they seemed chattier with each other, and I thought, Good for them.

It occurred to me that I was around more people than I'd been in a while, which I guess was since May, at Austen Riggs.

I thought about Andre, who was kind of a skank, and I kept wondering about the mysterious Levon Grady. Andre was slick as puppy shit, as this girl Suzy, at McLean, used to say. Whatever he was, Levon Grady was not puppy shit.

So Wednesday, ten in the a.m., my first class, if you could call it a class, I was sitting in Meg's office, in one of the big overstuffed chairs. Meg asked me if I'd written anything more, and I said, A little, and she said, Wanna show us?

Must I?

She laughed. I think that's part of the deal, she said. But if you want to wait a week or two to let it cool down, that's good with me.

If I wait a week or two I might delete it.

So maybe don't think and just hit send.

I'll try to try, I said.

She leaned back in her rolling desk chair and said, You

know how when you're a kid and you're dipping a toe in the water and they tell you to just jump in, or how they say just pull the Band-Aid off fast?

I nodded.

It works, she said.

It was five past, and still no Levon, and Meg said, Yesterday go okay?

Yeah, I think this might be okay, I said.

Then we didn't say anything for a minute or two, and then there was a soft tapping on the door.

Mr. Grady, enter, Meg said.

She stood up and quickly hugged him, and I stood up, and he was nothing like the way I'd thought.

For one thing, I'm pretty tall, almost five eight, and he was way taller than me, six two or three. He had wide, square shoulders, but was otherwise lean, and he had dark hair that wasn't long, but was loose and kind of curly and unruly and had hints of red in it. He wore glasses with brown frames that had wire on the bottom of the glass to hold the lenses in, kind of like '60s businessman glasses.

He wore a white short-sleeved shirt with the top button buttoned, and black khaki pants and really beat-up black Docs. I only looked briefly at his face, but his eyes were brown, and he was handsome. Jesus, he was handsome. Not pretty, not model handsome, but this slightly wide nose, and gorgeous lips, and his eyes looked at me a second and then away.

So, Sam, he said. So. Here we are.

He slouched onto the couch, and I sat too straight in the chair, and I said, Nice to meet you, Levon, and then I wanted to kick myself because that's what people at Groton said.

I might have been blushing, but I looked quickly over at him, and he was looking down at his shoes and smiling. Not smirking.

He said, I loved, Say here her / feet rose.

He kept looking at his shoes. Say here her, he repeated. Just lovely.

Six

~~~~~~~

Elliot

I didn't know him well, and this whole thing took about a minute, maybe two minutes in all, but it was one of the most amazing, awesome things I ever saw. Even though it took place six years ago, in late September, our first month in middle school, in sixth grade, I can see it all now like it was a day or a week or a month ago. I don't think it's something I'll ever forget.

As sixth graders, we were the new kids, just out of grade school, which was kindergarten to fifth, then middle school, which was sixth to eighth, then high school, which was ninth to twelfth.

So there were four different lunch blocks, E, F, G, and H, and the grades were all jumbled together at lunch, depending on your schedule. I think E started at eleven twenty, you had about thirty minutes, and so on.

I should also say that I'd gone to school at Fall Creek

Elementary all the way with Levon Grady, and though I wasn't real friendly with him—nobody was real friendly with him—I liked him, and thought he was a nice kid. He kept to himself, he was real smart, and he never bothered anybody.

He was also really tall, and wore glasses, and had curly hair, and even though he was skinny, he had broad shoulders, and he looked kind of skinny-strong, the way a swimmer looks, and he moved kind of fluidly, like an athlete, though he didn't play sports.

I didn't either. In fact, nobody in my family was interested in sports in any way, except for one thing. My parents loved Muhammad Ali, and we had a copy of *When We Were Kings*, the documentary about the Rumble in the Jungle, the famous fight in Zaire between George Foreman and Ali. My parents loved Ali's refusal to fight in the Vietnam War, and his courage and wit and how smart he was. I guess, too, they thought he was an amazing boxer, even though they didn't like or approve of boxing.

Anyway, by the time I was in sixth grade, I'd seen *When We Were Kings* about five times. How the massive Foreman was supposed to destroy Ali with these punches that hit like cinder blocks. That Ali was too old, outclassed, and just couldn't stand up to Foreman's thunderbolts. But Ali leaned way back on the ropes, the Rope-a-Dope, and let Foreman land body blow after body blow, and leaned his head back, and Foreman almost never hit Ali in the head. Finally, Foreman was punched out, and Ali started counter-punching with these incredibly hard, fast, and accurate shots to Foreman's head.

Well, during E-block lunch, there was a kid, an eighth grader, named Jason Slough. He was a big beefy kid who might have played football or something, and he always sat with his buddies near where some of us sixth graders sat. I don't know why, but he seemed to hate Levon, and almost from the first week of school, he'd been giving him a hard time. Bumping into him in the halls on purpose (har-har), and sitting during lunch and saying, Hey, LePussy, LeFaggot, what's for lunch today? It happened every E-block lunch.

Hey, LeShit, you cornhole your friends this weekend? Or you don't have no friends?

Aren't you some kind of freak, LeRetard? Go to special classes?

Jason Slough had a lot of acne, and a round red face, and he always wore a baseball cap on backward, and Timberlands that weren't laced all the way up. He was probably the same height as Levon, but he must have weighed close to twice as much.

I don't think many people liked him, and I think people liked Levon if they thought of him at all.

Isn't Levon a hillbilly name? Don't all hillbillies fuck their sisters and mothers? Slough taunted him on one day in particular.

There was silence for a moment or two. This was a Tuesday, I think.

Then Levon put his sandwich down, and stood up, and said, Okay, shitbird.

Jason Slough stood up, and there was a space between the tables, and a whole lot of people stood up and there was a thick circle of people around them. They put their hands up, and Jason kind of leaned back, then forward, and took this huge George Foreman swing at Levon's head. Levon stepped back, leaned his head back like Ali, and the punch missed by at least six inches.

Then Levon moved his feet, stepped forward, and while Slough was off balance, Levon Grady threw this hard punch that landed square on the side of Jason's face. It shocked him, you could tell. But before he could get his balance, Levon moved his feet again, stepped forward again, and threw a right that seemed to have every ounce of his weight, from his toes to his fist, behind it. The punch landed in the middle of Jason's face, and there was a cracking sound, and you could see Jason's legs wobble like he was drunk, and he just crumpled to the linoleum floor.

People were screaming, and teachers were rushing in.

Levon picked his backpack up, and I heard he went to the principal's office, and that was the end of Levon Grady and regular public schools.

I think Jason's mom tried to make a fuss, and threatened to sue, but a lot of people told about all the things Jason had been saying to Levon since the start of school. Jason had to wear a mask around school for his nose, and I kind of felt sorry for him.

He was just a bully, and now what was he? Just a prick who'd had his ass handed to him by a sixth grader.

Levon Grady was a boy of talent and mystery. He rode into the sunset like the Lone Ranger, wearing not a mask, but glasses.

Hi-yo, fucking Silver!

Seven

~~~~~~

Levon

I would've been there on time—I hate being late for anything—but just as I was walking out the door, my mom texted me and said she had forgotten to feed the cats. So I fed the cats, and they were swarming me like vultures, and I kept having to elbow them off the counters, especially when I cracked open the wet food. Honestly, they're like lions on the Serengeti with a fresh-killed gazelle or something.

The school was only four or five blocks away, but I was still about seven minutes late, and when I knocked and went in, she was sitting on the edge of one of the big chairs like she was at a tea party, spine like steel. She stood up, and she was quite tall and had this mass of light brown hair piled on the back of her head with silver combs to hold it there. She had wide-set brown eyes, big eyes, a long, thin nose, and perfect teeth.

She was almost gorgeous, but five out of ten people would say she was slightly strange-looking, nose too long or thin, mouth a little wide, and she was wearing an almost mannish shirt or blouse, long sleeved, with the top button buttoned, which made me think, Shit, my top button is buttoned too.

But her shirt was buttoned at the cuffs, and she wore black cargo pants, and Birks, and the thing that got me, that made me feel a little sad for her, was that she had this thin tan suit jacket over the shirt, and the sleeves of the suit jacket were rolled back once.

I thought, Cutter.

We sat down and I started saying how I loved her poem, especially, say here her / feet rose.

She blushed and said thank you. And I said it was lovely, the alliteration, the languid through / white summer.

You don't expect the white summer, you expect it to be green, of course, I said. Then I paused.

I turned to her, and she looked at me, still blushing. She had very fair skin.

I'm sorry. This must be embarrassing you, I said.

No, it's kind, she said, looking at her toes curled in her Birks.

Meg didn't say anything for a while. Meg watched both of us. She looked at me a few moments, then she looked at Sam. Meg was big on silence. She called it Quaker Silence.

You were silent, and things came out of the silence. God or grace came from the silence. Stillness.

We must have sat a minute or two in silence but it felt like a half hour. Finally I said, Sam, Meg has this thing about silence. That it's cool if there's silence. Kind of like a Quaker meeting. That grace and God can come from the stillness.

I'm good with that, Sam said.

It's not necessarily religious, Meg said. It's putting up with the anxiety. It's finding what Eliot called the still point in the turning world. Or Keats called it negative capability: the ability to be in mysteries, doubts, and uncertainties without the irritable reaching for fact or reason.

We were quiet a few seconds, then Meg said, You, Sam, sent Levon a poem, I gather, and Levon, you sent Sam something I've not been privy to. You've also had some idea, some sense, that this whole project might take place in cyberspace.

She looked at Sam, then at me.

Am I correct?

We both looked at Meg, then at each other. Sam had a hint of a smile.

Well, I said, we weren't exactly sure. I mean, it's all been kind of amorphous.

Sam?

I didn't exactly know.

How about we set some ground rules, because this is a kind of senior honors project, Meg said.

We did some more silence.

Which means that it counts as two courses a term. Sixteen credits.

Before you duck and run, you only have to take two other courses. So you'll have plenty of time. We'll meet twice a week here, in my office. Wednesdays at ten a.m., and Fridays at two p.m.

And as much as I know you're each disinclined to show, to share your work, I am making it a requirement of this course, that within a week of writing something, you send it to both Levon and me, or Sam and me.

And to help make it easier to open up, rule number one is that nobody else is to see your work, now or ever, unless all three of us agree.

Meg stopped, and I watched Sam look at the floor. Then Sam looked at me, and held my eyes, and I wasn't sure what she was seeing. Can I trust you? Are you like everyone else? Who are you, Levon Grady, and what is this place? She looked angry and scared, and she looked like she was pleading for something, but I didn't know what it was.

Then I looked at Meg. She had been watching us.

This could be a hundred pages, Sam said.

Yes, Meg said. But much of it will be accounts written or

emailed or transcribed by other people. And you have close to ten months to work on it.

And try not to think of it as just you working on this thing alone. It's you and Levon and me. We're all pulling this cart together. We're in it together, every step, every trudge, every stumble along the way.

Sam had sat back in her chair, and her legs were straight out in front of her. They were long as willows, and I noticed her arms were really long, and she had wonderful hands. Long, straight, strong fingers.

But I'm such a fuck-up, Sam said in this oddly flat way. As though she was talking to someone else.

We did some silence.

I've never finished anything, she finally said.

Then she pulled her legs up under her and turned away from us.

We're all fuck-ups, Meg said. Which is to say, we make mistakes, we fail at some things, we do better at some things. We're human beings.

I certainly am, I said.

Sam looked at me.

I'm a fuck-up. Majorly, I said.

I thought you were gonna say you were a human being, Sam said, and she laughed, then we all laughed.

I mean, I'm not always sure of that, I said. I have the basic attributes.

The arms, the legs, the hair, the heart, Sam said. She grinned slyly. You got your liver, you got your kidneys, you got your brains, eyes, ears, pancreas, she said in this Boston accent.

And don't forget the fingers and toes, your opposable thumb. Where would you be without your opposable thumb, I said.

We were riffing a little, having, you could almost say, fun.

Meg said, And what did you send Sam, Levon?

Oh, just this thing about an old lady across the street dying, I said. Just something I had just happened to have written.

You want me to tell about it? Sam asked.

It was really just something—

I'll tell, if that's okay, Sam said.

And she started to describe it in detail, as if she'd read it five times. She said it was very well written, very fluid, even elegant, and it was about these three people in their sixties who had lived across the street from me my whole life, and who hardly went out, and who weren't related as far as I could tell. She told about me seeing Mr. Smithie being taken out on a stretcher maybe a half dozen times over the years, usually at night, and how he was very short and very fat. And every time I thought he'd die, that this would be his last ride.

Then his mom wrote Levon an email, Sam said, that one of the two women who lived there had died and he hadn't even noticed, and how strange and sad that was. How he lived across the street from them his whole life and barely noticed them, how they kept the shades drawn, and how you hardly ever saw them. They kept to themselves.

It was sad, and it was such a curious thing to write about, such an interesting thing to notice, Sam said.

What struck you most? Meg asked.

Well, the writing, Sam said. And how Levon noticed things and thought about things, and how he was both really curious and really sad.

We were silent for a minute.

Anything else? Meg asked.

Well, there was one other thing that struck me, but this may be me. I've spent so much time with shrinks. I don't want to overanalyze everything.

Levon? Meg looked at me.

Sure.

It occurred to me that Levon, on some level, whether he was aware of it or not, was so curious, and empathized so deeply, maybe because he identified with the old people. I mean, they seemed to have had no friends or visitors, and they kept their shades drawn, and they might have kind of peeked out at the world from behind their curtains, just as Levon peeked out and saw the old man getting taken away in an ambulance. I wondered if he wondered what that life was like, and if he was maybe a little drawn to it, and a little scared that he could become like that. Afraid of being someone who peeked out at the world from behind veils.

I just looked at her looking at the floor, and I thought, Holy shit. OMG. Where did this girl come from?

We had a long Quaker Silence. Two minutes. Five minutes. We waited a long time, and I felt like I was being seen as I had never been seen. It was uncanny. Uncomfortable and wonderful at the same time.

Finally Sam said, I'm sorry if that's out of line. I always read way too much into everything.

Levon? Meg said.

I'm startled, I said very quietly. I wasn't really aware at the time I was writing it. But yeah. Yeah. That's it. That's got to be there. That is there. It's all over it.

Then we were silent, and something very strange happened, like it was happening to someone else. Like it was happening from far away. I felt stricken and pale. My hands were shaky.

All at once, I felt sad, but I felt relieved too, as though someone had finally seen me. From nowhere.

But Meg came over and sat next to me on the couch. She put her arm around me, and then she motioned for Sam to come over and sit on the other side of me. Sam didn't put her arm around me, but she put her long, beautiful hand on my wrist, and we sat there for two or three minutes.

It's good sometimes, Meg said, to get found.

Then they went back to their seats.

Meg said we were almost out of time, and that surprised me, because it felt like we'd just been in there a half hour. But it also felt like we'd been there half the day too. Maybe it was all those Quaker Silences. All that stillness and grace.

She said, I've drawn up contracts for both of you to sign. It basically says what we talked about. Meet twice a week, turn in at least one hundred pages in June, and absolute confidentiality. What we say and write stays between the three of us. No exceptions.

We each signed down at the bottoms of the pages, and we each got a copy.

And how about you two send me what you've already sent each other? And maybe try to write a little more for Friday? Anything. Just get the writing muscles moving.

We were standing at Meg's desk, and she was easily the shortest.

She handed us each cards with her telephone number and email address and, down at the bottom, she wrote in her cell phone number.

Why don't you give each other your cell numbers and stuff?

We did, and then we stood, and Meg said, Okay, let's bring it in.

I don't think Sam knew what Meg was talking about. But Meg pulled us into this tight three-way hug. Sam was stiff and awkward, and then Meg said, Relax, and Sam didn't so much relax, but her grip grew really strong, like rope, and it was as though she was hugging the two of us as if she meant it.

Then I said, Every year, Meg's gotten a little shorter.

Meg said, Every year, Levon's become more of a wiseass.

We broke and Meg said, We good?

Yeah, I said. Absolutely.

Sam said, I think so. As long as I didn't push it too far.

I looked at her, leaned close, and said, Not a bit. The Dude abides.

Then we both smiled, and at that moment I thought, She's not sort of a little, almost odd-looking. She's stop-your-blood, render-you-mute gorgeous. And she was half again as clear-eyed and sharp as anyone my age I'd ever come across. Which made me feel like skipping for joy and running away at the same time. And that was wonderful and scary in a way I don't think I'd ever known.

I could almost hear Meg say, You've finally met your match, Levon Grady.

Eight

~~~~~~~~~

Nathan

If you know Roslindale, then you probably know Boston.
It's a neighborhood of the city, about five miles from downtown, bordered by Mattapan, Hyde Park, Jamaica Plain, and
is a mixture of small single-family houses with chain-link
fences surrounding the tiny yards, two-family houses, and
an occasional three-decker, particularly near Mattapan.
Roslindale is a step or two up from South Boston, two steps
up from Dorchester, and two and a half steps up from
Roxbury.

So I grew up in Roslindale, and most of the kids I graduated high school with went to the army or navy or marines,
or jail, or they took the civil service exam to get on with the
post office or the fire department or the city. Or they became alcoholics or addicts, which is kind of a full-time job.
I went to UMass Boston, in Dorchester, built on a former

dump, situated not far from the always-congested Southeast Expressway.

My old man was a mail carrier, my mom was taken by cancer when I was sixteen, and I remember, in the last year of her life, how she said to my brother Bobby and me, over and over, Make something of yourselves. She must have said it a hundred times.

Maybe it was how skinny and gray she'd become, and how it was like she was gone before she was dead, but it made an impression on me. That, and how we knew, she knew, Bobby and I knew, that our dad could have been so much more. He worked hard. He went out in all kinds of weather. But at night, he read books. He listened to classical music. He read Tolstoy and Dostoevsky, and he read Plato. He loved Bach and Vivaldi, and this morning show on public radio called *Morning Pro Musica*. It had a guy who had a really deep voice and who spoke very slowly. Dad called him Robert J.

Bobby took the civil service exam and got on the fire department, but I went to UMass. I was seventeen, and it was odd because it was so much easier than high school in so many ways. You had a class or two or three each day, and then you could go home, or spend your time in the computer labs or the library, and the best thing was that there were no knuckleheads. No spitballs. No assholes in the back of the class with their Red Sox caps on backward, snapping gum, saying, Hey, Vash, ya mothah have any kids that lived? Hey, Vash, good to see ya back in men's clothes.

I was taking mostly math and computer science classes, and the professors were good. They weren't just punching the clock. You got your syllabus at the start of the semester, you knew what was expected, and it was clear and simple.

I knew I might not be the smartest kid in every class, but I was absolutely sure that nobody anywhere, ever, would outwork me. And that was my great strength, and of course, my great weakness. I never ever forgot where I came from, even later, when I was sitting on the top floors of the very, very best places. It consumed me sometimes.

I took precalculus, and basic programming, and a writing class, and American history, and first semester I got three As and an A-minus. I remember when the grades came in the mail, and I opened them, and it was my birthday, December 21, and my dad came in from work. It was dark out already. He was taking his coat off in the front hall, and I turned the hall light on, and after he hung his coat up he turned to me and I handed him the sheet with the grades.

What's this? he said.

Then he read, and I swear, there were not quite tears in his eyes. But almost, and I think that was from the cold.

But he said, Nathan. Then he paused, and he read again. And he said, It's your birthday too.

Let's each get a beer, he said.

Then we were both sitting in the parlor, and he said, I'm not a bit surprised. Not one bit.

We sipped. Then he smiled and said, What's with the A-minus?

First semester sophomore year, I met Professor Ira Rosen, who had really and truly given up a tenure-track job at Harvard to come to UMass because he believed in public higher education. He said, Think of all those smart Jews at City College in the '30s and '40s who they wouldn't let into Columbia and Yale. Schmucks!

He came to UMass to help build math and business and computer-science departments.

After about six weeks in his computer programming class, he called me into his office, looked at my test score, which was 99 percent, and said, Are you a Jew, Nathan Vash?

Am I a what?

A Jew?

He was short and thick and bald, and wore thick rimless glasses.

Not that I know of.

What are you?

I was brought up Catholic, and I think my mother was

Irish and my father was Ukrainian or Latvian or something.

They made him convert, the fucking Russians or Krauts, Rosen said.

He looked me over some more. What's your dad do?

Postal carrier.

Does he read books? Listen to music? Good music?

I nodded.

Classical music?

Like Bach? I said.

Jew, Rosen said. I knew it. With some Irish thrown in. Two exiled peoples. Your mother read?

She's dead. But she used to.

He looked down.

I'm sorry, he said.

From that time on, I was Ira's protégé, he was my rabbi. I took six classes with him, in advanced calculus, physics, computer programming, number theory, business applications, and a senior honors thesis on encryption and integers.

Ira's theory was that everything in the universe was absurdly simple and absurdly complex. It was all 01010101— only stretched out to infinity, and prime numbers were absurdly simple but with a diabolical twist. He said they drove brilliant men crazy.

In August, right before the start of senior year, he said, What'll it be next year, kiddo?

What do you think?

He smiled, then started to laugh. An old Jewish trick, he said, perfected by Freud. You answer a question with a question and they think you're wise. Very wise.

Well, maybe grad school?

Okay. Where?

I shrugged.

What's your GPA?

Three-nine-something. Seven or eight.

You take the GMATs?

Seven-seventy.

How's the B-School sound?

The who?

Harvard Business School.

Me? UMass Boston. Roslindale.

You'd be the first.

Could I do it?

Shit, yes.

You'd get in, he went on. They'd love to see a kid make that kind of jump, and you'd kick ass academically. The big thing is the social shit. All the arrogant shits with the social skills, Choate, Exeter, Yale, Williams, the clothes, the cars, the clubs, the confidence. But I'd like to see you do a Ph.D. after the M.B.A. Give you more flexibility, if you got tired of just making money.

Should I apply anywhere else?

He gave me one of his sly smiles. No need, he said. I think you're a lock.

No BU, UMass Amherst?

Fuck 'em, kid. You're going all the way. To the moon, Alice! And he made this punching gesture, which I didn't realize till years later was an imitation of Jackie Gleason in *The Honeymooners*.

So the B-School was the only place I applied, and I got in, and I got a full ride, which was unusual. Harvard had a great deal of money, and they give a great deal in scholarship money, but far less to B-School students, in part because the average incoming student is twenty-seven, and has some money saved, and will soon be making a great deal more.

But Ira Rosen must have made some phone calls, must have talked about UMass, about Roslindale, about my father the mail carrier, and he must have convinced them I walked through fire and then across water.

I took all the usual first-year stuff, finance, marketing and technology, operations management, and a bunch of other stuff, but I got very lucky because I did my Field Immersion Experiences for Leadership Development at Fidelity in Boston, which was big at the time, but not yet huge. And I studied their security systems.

I later did a six-week FIELD at Bank of Boston, and that was where I met Vera Van Resse. Vera was in her first year at the B-School, and I was in my second.

Vera was about five eight, and had brown-blond hair that was always coiled, or held with silver combs, and she wore silk scarves, even in the summer. She had very fair skin, and green eyes, and high cheekbones, and she seemed to know she was a knockout, but she didn't seem to care. She was friendly with everyone, and during that first summer, she'd come to me with questions, always with computer questions. I'd answer them, and one time, near lunch, she said, Don't you ever eat lunch? And I said I brown-bagged it.

She didn't know what that meant, and when I said I brought my own lunch, she laughed, and said, I think I at least owe you a lunch for answering all my questions.

I seemed reluctant, and she said, The building won't collapse without you holding up the walls for an hour.

Vera and I went to a diner, and I've got to say, I liked her, and I think she liked my reluctance, that I wasn't hitting on her.

So you're the boy wonder from UMass Boston, she said, and I said, Roslindale, ever been there?

She said she'd heard of it, that it was near Mattapan and Jamaica Plain—but no, she'd never had the pleasure.

Such as it is, I said. You're from?

Back Bay, then Williams. Plus a house on the Vineyard. Ever been there?

I shook my head. You will, she said. But you've become

kind of locally famous, and pretty fast, she said. A real comer. Top five percentile.

The B-School loved percentiles and statistics, and everyone seemed to know where everyone else stood in the class.

And Peter Lynch is reputed to have his eye on you, she said.

Peter Lynch was just getting really, really famous at Fidelity Magellan, the way Warren Buffett and Bill Gates were famous. I had had lunch with Mr. Lynch and two vice presidents at Fidelity once, and everyone seemed to know it.

So that's where you'll be next year? she asked.

Nope.

Where?

MIT. Ph.D. in computer science. Hacking, worms, viruses, security. Two more years.

So somehow, in this unlikely way, Vera Van Resse of the Back Bay and Martha's Vineyard and Nathan Vash of Roslindale became a couple.

The first time I met her parents, went to their house on Marlborough Street between Dartmouth and Clarendon, I realized just how different the world I was entering actually was. It was a full brownstone, with marble steps, and it was so much bigger inside than I could have imagined. There were old paintings, and there was, I believe, a real Jackson Pollock, and there was Jack Van Resse and Vivian, and they were gracious and kind, and they sat us down in the upstairs parlor—I remember Jack called it a *parlor*—and Vivian brought in cocktails on a tray, and Jack positively beamed at me.

I understand you're putting off Peter Lynch for a few years, Jack said, and I said I thought it would give me more flexibility.

So MIT? Vivian asked. How many years will that take?

I hope two, I said. I've done a lot of the preliminary work. Maybe two and a half.

By gosh, Jack said.

Nathan's a grinder, Vera said, and we laughed.

When Vera came to meet my dad, she could not have been more kind, more natural. She acted as though she'd been in Roslindale every other weekend, and that tiny yards with chain-link fences and Mary on the half shell were commonplace.

We had come, in fact, to tell him we were getting married. We had moved into an apartment in Cambridgeport together in mid-August, just before I started MIT. We had brought a bottle of wine, and we drank it in the parlor, out of juice glasses. Vera had kissed my father on the cheek, and I realized in heels she was as tall as he was, or that he had shrunk after so many years of lugging mail.

He was shy. Then she stood up and started looking through his bookcases and CD collections.

Trollope, she said. *Buddenbrooks, The Magic Mountain. Nostromo.* You're a reader, Mr. Vash.

It passes the time, he said.

You're a serious reader, she said. Chekhov. *Middlemarch.*

Then she reached the CDs. Bach, Schumann, Chopin, Fauré. Respighi, Puccini.

Vera got him talking about Chekhov, of all things, how he got life onto the pages. No guns, he said, no car chases or horse chases, just basic everyday life, and there was never a false word, a false moment. At first you thought, Is that it? Then you reread and reread, and you realized, That's what life is.

We got married, I finished the Ph.D. in two and a half years, Vera finished the B-School and started working for First Boston, then Credit Suisse after the merger of the banks, and I worked at Fidelity.

I did some work in the financial sectors, but by then Fidelity was a giant, managing about one trillion dollars in investments, and all of that traveled by wire. Telephone, computer, wireless wire, and there were tens of thousands, hundreds of thousands of transactions a day. And where there were vast amounts of money, there were hackers. Very smart, very savvy people who could create worms and viruses, who could find keys to unlock doors, who could hack their way into our systems.

So this became my specialty, and I was good at it. I was

good at encryption, at firewalls, at usernames and passwords, at setting traps, hoops for hackers to jump through. Trips and traps. By the time I was twenty-eight, I was junior vice president, by thirty-one, senior vice president. When I was twenty-nine years old, I made over a million dollars a year, not counting my bonus. At thirty-three, I made three million dollars including bonuses.

And that's when everything started to change. Sometime between twenty-eight and thirty-three. We had Samantha, Vera left First Boston, we bought a three-million-dollar house in Chestnut Hill, and I was working seventy-hour weeks.

It was slow, and it was invisible and incremental, but we were going so fast in the slowness that we didn't notice how much things were changing. Like you looked in the mirror every day and didn't see anything different, but put two photos of the same face taken five years apart, and it was obvious. Time had moved.

We had obscene piles of money, a house that felt like a museum, and my daughter and wife, who I loved more than the world, were drowning in something I couldn't even name. It was so bad, I was working so much, I barely noticed they were drowning.

Nine

~~~~~~

Sam

At that first meeting, when I talked about how maybe Levon was seeing himself as the old people, not going out much, and peeking out at the world, and possibly ending up kind of alone and isolated and strange—and then there was silence, that stillness, and then the stricken look on his face—I thought, You asshole, Sam. You absolute blundering asshole. What have you done? I wanted to crawl into a closet.

But then something changed. Levon changed, or Meg let us sit with it in silence, and then at the end when Levon said, almost with glee, The Dude abides, I can't tell you what a wringer, a seesaw, a roller coaster of emotions I went through, all in about fifteen minutes.

It was like he was really, really sad, and I saw how terribly alone he was, and probably always had been. He was almost embarrassed but glad at the same time to be seen, to be found out. That someone had looked closely and carefully enough, and he could finally exhale.

I also felt a little bit ashamed of myself, because I had written my enigmatic little poem, and what was he or anybody supposed to make of that? I mean, he said nice things, he noticed what was interesting and good in it, but I gave him almost nothing to work with.

So I thought I should start with Groton, which was just about a year ago, and how much I didn't want to go, and what a bad, awful idea it was. I'd had over a full good year at this place called the Crafts School, which was pretty much a fancy sort of Clock School. But Vera's dad had gone to Groton, and maybe her uncle and grandfather too, and no one thought about how terrible it would be for me to enter as a junior, when everyone else had already found their friends and groups.

So Grandmother and Grandfather pushed, and asshole Mom really pushed, saying this would show just how far I'd come, and how the previous fifteen years had really been nothing, had been kind of a big mistake, a patch of stormy weather, and now I could go to Groton and then Smith or Princeton or Swarthmore.

Dad wasn't crazy about the idea, I remember. He kept saying, She's doing great. Don't fix it if it ain't broke, but he wasn't around much, even though he was working for the Harvard Corporation by then, and wasn't nearly as busy.

The Crafts School was loose and easy, kind of how the Clock School turned out to be. I had been doing okay there. I didn't like the rigidity of regular fifty-minute classes.

So I took a bunch of tests that summer, and did very well, even in precalculus, and was accepted. Groton was beautiful in the summer—all this old red brick, and huge oaks and chestnuts. And no students around.

I moved in in late August for a week of orientation, mostly with younger kids, and a few other transfer students. And as soon as my parents drove away in Dad's black Benz, I thought, This is a mistake. This is a big and bad and stupid mistake, and I have no fucking way out of here.

There was chapel, and the pastor or minister, or whoever he was, welcomed us, and talked about the long proud history of Groton, and the tradition of Duty, Service, and Courage, and I swear to God it was as though he was getting us ready to go fight the Huns in the First World War.

There were dorms, in red brick, of course, two-story buildings in a semicircle, and then when the regular students came back, it was a nightmare. They had special names for each other—the Loomster, Otter, Feet, Cactus—and they had spent the summer on the Vineyard or some island off the coast of Maine, or in Italy, Morocco, Greece, building huts for poor people in Bolivia. Dude, that's major service points for Yale, some kid said.

They wore pale green and orange shorts, blazers and

ties, and by the first regular weekend of the semester, I bought a pint of vodka from a kid on the hall downstairs for twenty bucks. I just saw no way out of this awful world. I had no place in it. I was utterly trapped, and I wasn't thinking clearly. The world was black and white. While everybody was off at a movie or dance or playing video games in game rooms built for the sons and daughters of kings, I locked the bedroom door on myself. I had a cup, a pint of orange juice, my vodka, and an X-Acto knife.

I made a screwdriver with the vodka and juice, and drank slow enough so that I didn't throw up or spill anything, and the place was empty. The place was quiet.

Then after an hour or so, I was pretty drunk. When I tried to stand up, I nearly fell over. I sat on the edge of the bed, took my top off, took off my socks and jeans, so all I was wearing was a bra and panties. I remember they were both black, and I remember how pale my skin looked. I even took my watch and earrings off.

Then I went to the bathroom, which was en suite, with my drink and my blade. I turned the water in the shower on. When it was warm, but not too hot, I sat on the floor of the shower. I drank the rest of the screwdriver.

Then I leaned my head back against the wall of the shower, and thought, Well, here we are.

I picked up the X-Acto knife in my right hand, pressed

the blade deep into the inside of my left wrist, and drew it across. It stung like hell, and was bright, bright red. I knew I got the tendons, 'cause I could sort of feel my hand flapping.

But the blood was not gushing, just dripping pretty steadily, and I sat there and thought, Sam, you're so pathetic. You're such a fucking drama queen. I knew I hadn't hit a vein because veins spurt blood.

Then after a while, five minutes or a half hour, I either passed out or fell asleep.

Then there was just nothing, just blackness.

Then there was everything. Banging on the door. Loud bangs. People yelling, Samantha, Samantha, you in there? Then keys jangling and bright lights, and someone said, Oh, God, and there were about three or four people in the tiny bathroom.

Two were in blue uniforms, and one was in white, and I heard, Ambulance.

Someone else said, Elevate, direct pressure, and someone asked if there were pill bottles around, and another person said just vodka as far as she could see.

They got me on my feet and wrapped me in towels and a blanket, and put a towel in my hair. A woman in blue lifted me onto a stretcher, and there were kids staring on the stairs, and a lot more kids outside on the lawns, near the ambulance.

I didn't think anything, didn't feel anything. I was a pure black hole, just dense as matter could be, and someone held my left arm up the whole time.

They radioed the hospital that we were coming, and took my pulse and temperature and blood pressure, and I think they said the pulse was racing and the blood pressure was low. Or the pulse was low and the blood pressure was racing. I can't remember.

At the hospital, they got me into one of those curtained rooms, and they were very gentle. But I was falling deeper and deeper down and it was getting darker and darker. I was way down low where I could barely hear them. I was less than nothing. A fuck-up's fuck-up.

They had to get a plastic surgeon, to reattach the ligaments or tendons, or whatever the fuck I'd cut, and that took a while. For him to get there, and get his gear on. And when he was done there was a second doctor who did the outer skin, and by then it was pretty late. It was one or two.

Some social worker or nurse or someone asked me if I wanted to die, and I said, Yes, and she said, A beautiful girl like you, with everything to live for.

I thought, Lady, no offense, but you have no clue, no hint of an idea of what it feels like in the darkness.

Then they took me to a medical floor, then a psychiatric floor, and they shot me full of something that made me wicked tired. And I remembered reading how sometimes, because of a head injury or something, they'd have to put someone in a medically induced coma, and I thought that that was what I wanted. If I couldn't die, I wanted a coma. A long, long time under.

I barely talked for days. My dad and mom came, and flowers came, and nurses and doctors came, and after a day or four days, I was taken by ambulance to McLean, with a big white bandage around my left wrist, which made everything pretty obvious and boring and unambiguous.

I still said just about nothing, and within a week, I think, they started ECT. That had its own whole protocol, almost like you were going to surgery. No solid food after eight the night before, and only clear liquids until eleven, I believe it was. You had to answer all these questions about anesthesia: Could you climb stairs without getting winded? Any family history of sleep apnea? Any trouble breathing? And on and on.

I was still in a small dark place. A closed place. And I didn't want to leave. As long as it was quiet, as long as nobody came or went, as long as the world left me alone, I was good. Just keep it dark and keep it closed. I remembered these lines from the Psalms, Thou hast laid me in the lowest place, in darkness, in the deeps.

So they came for me early, and they put a needle in the back of my hand, and they said that I would be sedated, first with something called a benzodiazepine, to help me relax, and then with this white milky drug called propofol, which would put me to sleep. They put me on a gurney, and put a hairnet over my hair, but otherwise I kept my regular sleeping gear, my sweats, on.

They wheeled me into a room, and some young guy with the doctor thing over his hair said he was Dr. Someone, and they shifted me to another table.

I'm the anesthesiologist, he explained. I'll be with you the whole time. I'm giving you something to relax, and he injected something clear into the lead in the line on the back of my hand, and it was immediate, and, man, it was fast. I was swooning.

Then he took this syringe with milky stuff in it, and he said, We call this milk of magnesia, and he injected it, and in one, two seconds, I was gone.

I woke up in a comfortable, deep leather recliner, and I was floating slowly and I could have been on the way to France or Japan or Patagonia—it was all good with me.

After a while they wheeled me back to my room, and there was Chloe, and I think I slept most of the day.

But looking back, and even though I didn't know it then, someone or something had sent a thin silky thread down the hole to me.

Ten

Noah

I had known Levon Grady for more than twelve years, since kindergarten at Fall Creek, but to say you knew Levon was a highly relative claim. Nobody, I think, really knew Levon, except maybe his mother, or possibly Meg Goldman at the Clock School. But in another sense, everybody knew Levon, because he was so big and handsome, and he was incredibly interesting and odd.

Brilliant and mysterious, this mass of contradictions, and in some curious way, I felt a special affinity to him, though people would laugh to hear me say that.

I was small and skinny and nondescript. But I kind of had this secret life, playing the cello, which almost no one knew about, and I was really good at it, and I played, not at school, but on weekends in a string quartet, and summers at music camp, and at home every night. It was my private, eccentric love.

I kind of kept it secret because I loved it so much that if people knew about it, and someone made fun of the cello, or Bach or Vivaldi, it would almost be more than I could handle, and I might want to give it up. It was just too precious to let anyone know.

I know that's not rational, but if nobody knew, then no one could ridicule it, and thus threaten it in any way.

I thought of myself as bright, and interesting in my way, so if I looked at myself in a fun-house mirror, I might see Levon Grady. Someone who was really bright, who was tall, had broad shoulders, was handsome, but who was very shy, and kept to himself, and who went unnoticed.

Although Levon could hardly be unnoticed. Because of the way he looked, because he was very quiet and withdrawn, although once in a while, when the teacher would call on him, and it was a question or subject that interested him, he would talk like a volcano and the lava would flow. And during gym, he'd kick the ball over the fence, or run the mile way faster than anybody else. But he was always nice and polite, in his very withdrawn way, his nondescript way, to everybody.

Nobody, not teachers, not his fellow students, knew what to make of him. Except the girls, of course. They were all, at least a half dozen, always in love with him. Sometimes they hated him, at least one or two, because he was so oblivious, so indifferent to them. Other girls would dare their friends to run up and kiss him or hand him notes proclaiming, I guess, their love, or a friend's love, for him. But Levon never reacted.

And as we got a little older, into third or fifth or whatever grade, there were rumors about his mother, who was a neuroscientist and an expert on serial killers, and about the fact that Levon didn't have a father. Or one that he knew of, and that his mother would never tell him who his father was.

Now that was weird. Why would that be? Wouldn't that have to be the darkest secret, and wouldn't that have to mean that Professor Grady, during research in graduate school, had gotten pregnant by one of the serial killers? Why else keep such a secret?

Nobody kidded or taunted Levon about that. He was too distant, although thinking about it now, maybe that was why he was so distant. He was also so big and strong and a little bit weird that we were all just a little bit afraid of him.

I mean, he got invited to birthday parties and things like that, and in the very early grades, maybe kindergarten and first or second grade, he went to a few, but he usually stayed in a corner with a computer, or built a Lego fort more or less alone. And he never had birthday parties himself.

Professor Grady was tall and beautiful and kind of scary,

kind of intimidating. Like she was the opposite of warm and friendly and approachable. You'd see her very rarely, partly because Levon lived only a block and a half from the school, so from real early, maybe even kindergarten, he walked to school on his own.

None of this is to say that Levon was a freak or a complete weirdo. He knew everyone's name, and said hello, and made funny little comments, and played chess with other kids during lunch break. And one time, I think in third or fourth grade, we had this really nutty ADD kid named Bobby, who couldn't sit still and was pretty mean, and he kind of flipped, and knocked over his desk, and picked up a chair and was actually threatening Ms. Evans, the teacher, with it, and Levon grabbed the chair, and got between Bobby and Ms. Evans, and he very calmly held Bobby by the shoulders and said, Bobby, you've got to chill. C'mon, buddy, and then things went crazy; the aides and principal were there, and they got Bobby out of the room.

I sometimes got the feeling that Levon wanted to be just a regular kid, but somehow, because of how he looked, and because he was so bright, and maybe because of his mother and not knowing his father, he couldn't.

And then the big thing, of course, was in sixth grade. Unlike a lot of people who claim to have been there, I was actually sitting about three seats down from Levon, and I'd been hearing this Slough idiot taunting Levon for weeks.

I didn't know what Levon would do, but I almost felt sorry for Slough, because I knew Levon, in a way, and I knew how calm and smart and strong he was.

It was over in, like, a minute, if that. Slough didn't come close to hitting Levon, and with two powerful shots, Slough was on the ground with a broken nose. And Levon was so calm. He just picked up his backpack and went to the principal's office.

He was out of school a year, and later, when I heard he was going to the Clock School, it kind of made me want to go there too. I wanted to go to this tiny school, play the cello in secret, and be around people like Levon Grady. Who was different, but not a weirdo. He was the same Levon, only he didn't stick out so much. Everyone at the Clock School was at least a little bit odd. Levon was just shy, and trying to find his way, and sometimes he'd even stop and say to me, How's it going, and pat me on the back. I could almost call him a friend.

Well, not exactly a friend. But someone I knew and trusted. Someone I knew I could count on in a weird way. Someone who would understand about me being in a string quartet, if I told him, and why I thought Bach was almost a god.

People would laugh if they heard scrawny Noah say this, but I almost saw Levon as a compatriot, as a very distant soul mate.

Eleven

~~~~~~~

Levon

Reading what she wrote about Groton, about trying to leave the world—it messed me up, far more than other things she'd written. I was sitting on the futon, my bed on the third floor at home, and the only light came from the computer, and I could tell right away, from the first lines, that this was gonna be serious. That she wasn't withholding anything. This wasn't lick smooth my shadow from her first little poem. She was putting it out there.

Maybe because without even trying she had seen through me to the loneliness, the peeking out from behind curtains, to the fear, and she'd seen how that had gotten to me, she'd seen me trembling, so she felt she had to put herself out there. She owed it to me, she owed it to Meg, and most of all, she owed it to herself.

Because she was braver than I could ever be. She was

stronger than she realized. Maybe she had nothing to lose, or maybe she trusted us. I don't know.

But I sat there in the dark, pillows against my back, the pale laptop on my knees, and as I read I was trembling. There was all the drama, all the tension, all the life-and-death stuff, but it was so matter-of-fact.

I kept thinking, maybe saying out loud, maybe whispering, No, don't. No, please don't. But she couldn't, of course, hear. I kept pausing and looking up. I pushed my head back against the pillows, and I thought of her, how badly, thoroughly, utterly alone and black that must have been. And the release. Her hand flapping from the cut tendons, and I thought of her blood and warm water washing down the drain, and her head against the shower wall, and I said or thought, Sam, Sam, Sam, Sam. Oh, Jesus, Sam. Oh, fuck.

Then the voices, the pounding on the door, the keys, the elevate and direct pressure, and she would not leave the world. Going out on a stretcher and all those kids in orange and yellow shorts watching, and the ambulance and hospital, and I felt myself breathe, I felt the air going in and out of my lungs.

Then McLean. This beautiful sixteen-year-old kid. Her hand and wrist wrapped in white. And still deep, deep down. In shock and awe. Or numb from head to toe.

They must have tried all the meds for years and years.

Nothing had worked, I guess. So they go directly to ECT. Needle in the hand, knock her out. Propofol. And sort of waking in a daze. Volts of electricity to the brain. To this sixteen-year-old kid. Her lovely hair covered with a blue cap. Dense clouds filling her brain. Lightning bolts.

I looked out the windows on the far side of the room, beyond my desk, to the street, the streetlight, then I looked at the skylights, and the dark sky was cloudy. The ceiling was inclined, running under the roof, and down both sides of the lower parts of the walls were bookcases filled with books and clothes and CDs, and my little stereo system.

I wondered where she was. I closed the computer lid, and just lay there for a while and thought about her. It was early October, and leaves were just beginning to fall from the trees, and I felt for my flip phone. I thought of something, then chased it from my mind.

I wanted so badly to call her. It was ten thirty-seven, and I thought, I can't do that. It's too late. Then I thought, Email, text.

I'd never done something like that.

I got my wallet off the shelf next to my watch, and took out the Post-it where Meg had written Sam's email and phone number.

I opened the phone and thought, C'mon. Don't be a baby.

Then I thought, What are you gonna say?

Say what you feel, I told myself. Say you were moved. That you're really, really glad she's here.

Then I thought, I'll text to see if I can call. Maybe she'll be asleep.

I hit message, punched her number in, and wrote, Can I call you? This is Levon.

I waited about a minute, then hit send.

Right away, she wrote back, Of course.

Right now? I texted.

Why not?

You're not asleep or anything?

Wld I be texting you if I was?

Ok.

I dialed, and she said, You're funny, Levon.

How come?

Was I asleep? she said, and laughed.

Yeah, I guess that wasn't too shrewd of me.

No.

I guess I was nervous. I don't call people much.

I bet.

So—

So where are you?

At home. In my bedroom. In the attic. The third floor.

Hmmm. Me too. I live on the third floor too. I mean, that's where my bedroom is.

Cool.

So you just decided to call?

I just read your Groton piece.

Oh, God. Did you hate it?

Hate it?

Did you think it was pathetic?

No. Far from it. I just wanted to say, I'm very, very glad you're here. That you're alive and not dead.

Thanks. Me too.

And I could say more, but I won't. Just . . . great job.

Thanks.

Okay, I said. Good night.

And hung up.

I lay there in bed and thought of how awkward, how weird, I was. How maladroit. I thought of all the things that were in me, all the things I had wanted to say, and then thought of what I had said.

I'm glad you're not dead.

If I could have kicked myself in the ass, I would have. What a bonehead, a fuck-face, a weirdo. Why could I never get anything right? Always be a fuck-up?

Was I always gonna be like this? The loser, standing at the dance of life, looking in from the porch window, wondering how they all did it. Learned the steps, knew what to say, what not to say. Not worried that they'd jump out of their own scalded skin.

Twelve

~~~~~~

Vera

To say that I was unprepared for the birth of Samantha is to say that a fifth grader was unprepared for a college physics exam. I thought I was completely ready, utterly informed, had paid attention, gone to all the classes, read the books, and taken careful notes. But then: boom. I was in labor, the pains started, and it was like sliding down a very long descent into hell. We went to Brigham and Women's Hospital in Boston, of course, because, naturally, we had to have the best, and they put that bracelet on my wrist and took all my clothes, though I remember I got to keep my wedding ring and my socks. And I was a vessel, a big scalpel of pain, and my body was the waiting room for the arrival of the baby. I was the tunnel, and this was no tunnel of love. This was the tunnel of a remorseless struggle to get this child out into the world.

So what I got was, I believe, twenty-three hours of back

labor all the way, because she was head down all right, but facing the wrong way. A few times, twice, I think, a large, white-bearded man who seemed like Santa Claus came in and injected something into my spine, and that was miraculous, because the pain ceased. Completely. And for an hour, maybe two, I was, if not in heaven, not in Very Hell, and that was lovely.

I could feel the contractions, but they didn't hurt, but then after a while they began to hurt more, then more, then they were worse than ever, if that was possible. Finally, very early in the morning, the nurses, and Nathan, who'd been there the whole time, feeding me ice chips, urging me to take those useless breaths they taught us in baby classes, decided on a cesarean. And they shaved my pubic hair, and put needles in the backs of my hands, and shifted me to a gurney, and I thought, Wheel me to the morgue, baby, take me anywhere but here.

Then I was in the OR, and the Santa Claus man took me to Utter Heaven, and then they set a bunched, large object on my chest, and said, Isn't she a beautiful girl?

And I thought, What is this? Is this a person? My child? My Samantha? And everyone was happy, everyone was jolly, except me.

I remember thinking, Vera, you are fucked up. What is wrong with you?

Let's have some bonding, some glow, some love.

But they took her away to examine her, and they did stuff to me, including delivering the afterbirth, sewing my poor torn vagina and my flaccid belly, and they said she was eight pounds, three ounces, a big girl, and I remember that her head seemed as large as a hairless Saint Bernard, and that she wiggled a good deal, and had gray eyes, and seemed all head and legs, elbows and knees.

We were home in a day or two at most, and breast-feeding was a nightmare. She just wouldn't take to the breast, would latch on for a few seconds, would turn away, and cry and scream. I think we were at the pediatrician's every other day. Try the bottle, don't try the bottle because if you do there's no going back, and my mother said, All three of you—my two brothers and I—were raised on the bottle and look at you. You're all fine.

My nipples were cracked and aching, the stitches were killing me, and I thought, This is not going well. What had we been thinking?

Samantha lost weight. She was under eight pounds, and finally, we supplemented with the bottle, and after a week it was all bottle, and that was another failure.

No natural childbirth, no breast-feeding, the kid would have been dead if this was two hundred years ago.

She cried, she was in distress, she writhed like someone was poking her with pins, she didn't sleep much, we didn't sleep much. We had a nanny, and if it hadn't been for her,

Margaret, and for Laura, who did weekends, I swear, I would not have made it. This child of mine would not be alive.

I guess I'd had this picture in my mind, Mother and Child, breast-feeding, in a rocking chair, in front of a fireplace, and our eyes are gazing with adoration at each other, and, sure, there are the jokes, the tired, frazzled parents, but basically it's a happy, hopeful time.

I mean, I look back and my mother and father were not exactly warm and hovering parents. They traveled a good deal, and we children were left with a nurse and nanny, and I don't much remember either of my parents even touching us but for the briefest peck on the cheek, but I thought that was what parents were like.

But I swear, I wasn't naïve. I had talked to plenty of parents of young children. They said it was tough. They said you never sleep. You lose your sex life, your social life. It's all about feeding and fluids, diapers and sleep. Keeping the poor child from screaming.

And Samantha had screams. A whole symphony, a band, a quartet, a quintet, a horn section, an ensemble, a wind section, a string section that could whisper or shriek—of crying. She could start low, and build slow, and she could go to full Wagner. Whatever was right or wrong with her, her lungs were fully developed and very powerful.

To this day, anywhere, in a store, the street, a park, when I hear a baby cry, I go into panic. It hits me somewhere deep in the brain stem, and I'm helpless and enraged, and I feel profoundly inadequate. I don't believe I will ever feel otherwise.

Colic, it's called, and she had massive colic. It's supposed to pass in a few months. In six months. She was supposed to sleep through the night in a few months, in six months. But I swear. It went on for more than a year. Could it have gone on for two years?

Did this kid somehow genetically hate me or something?

And then somewhere around a year and a half, two years, she grew silent. She was supposed to be saying, Gaga, Dada, Mama, but nothing. None of those bright bubbles of sound.

Through all this, I became a different person. Nathan tried to help. Nathan was good. He was patient. He was kind. But Nathan was working sixty, seventy hours a week, and then we got the house in Chestnut Hill, which was supposed to help everything. All that light and air. All those birds and trees and flowers.

And me complaining, me pissing and moaning, with full-time help. And I still couldn't handle it. What did regular people do? What did single mothers do? I hated myself for that too.

Originally I was supposed to go back to Suisse after three months, then we extended it another three months, and then I never went back. I became a failure. A person who saw a psychoanalyst three times a week, who took Prozac for postpartum depression, lorazepam for anxiety, and Ambien for sleep.

The shrink's office was at the side entrance of her big house in Newton, and she was matronly. Large breasts, hips, tall, quiet-spoken, and she had several African masks on the walls of her office. Of course. And where did we begin?

I barely remember, except that she took a lot of notes on a yellow legal pad those first few weeks. Father, mother, brothers, husband, daughter, education, work, depression, suicidal thoughts, sleep, diet, sex life, general health, and on and on.

So what brings you here? she asked, and I talked and cried and cried and talked, and our fifty minutes were up. See you Wednesday.

So it went for twelve, thirteen years. And I don't know what I got out of it. She rarely said much.

She'd ask, What about that?

Or, It's as though you're inviting us not to analyze that.

Or, You sound quite angry, quite resentful of Samantha.

No shit, Sherlock.

I became a person who didn't do or want very much. Except I shopped all the time. But I wanted my daughter not to die or hurt herself, though God knows, she tried.

We brought her to every specialist at Children's

Hospital—neurology, psychiatry, audiology, speech therapy. She had brain scans, MRIs of every part of her body.

They talked depression, Asperger's, anxiety disorder, personality disorder, ADD.

But one good thing we did, and we did it from around the age of two, when she stopped screaming and we were settled into Chestnut Hill, was read to her. During the day, before dinner, before bed. Even when Nathan was getting home at eight or nine, he'd check on her, and if she was still awake, he'd lie on her bed, sometimes still in his suit and overcoat, and they'd read *Frog and Toad*, *Owl Moon*, *Big Red Barn*, Beverly Cleary, Katherine Paterson, and later Harry Potter.

It was as though she became a different child then. Quiet, attentive, and we could even see her mouth the words along with us.

She did begin to speak, of course, but very quietly and in a whispery voice at first, sometime around the age of three. And she spoke in full sentences, and she had quite a vocabulary. She even smiled once in a while, and she had gorgeous blond hair that had wavy curls. Her nose was long, but Nathan said, I guarantee you she'll grow into it.

At school, beginning with preschool, she was always a loner. *Does not play well with others*. That appeared on just about every report we ever got. And because so much of school at that age was about socialization, we were off to more doctors, more diagnoses.

At one point we toured a school for Asperger's kids, and the kids, such beautiful children, crouched or stood alone or ranted to themselves as though to some internal audience, and we both said, No. Not Samantha.

My analyst asked, Denial?

And I said, No. It wasn't right.

We did eventually get her to schools with resources for bright kids with special needs. She tested extremely well. And by that time we had enough money for a lifetime, and Nathan had moved to Harvard, in part because it would be fewer hours, and more time for Samantha. And things settled for a year or so.

Then we thought, Groton. Small. Intimate. Caring. A great deal of individual attention.

Then the Groton disaster, a year of hospitals, and here we are, like a whirlwind, Dorothy's house set down in Oz, and I'm actually teaching a class in finance at Cornell.

I know a lot of this is on me. Me, we, all of us, have miles and years to go.

But every now and then, say in the morning, looking out at the flowers and trees in the backyard, I get this strange momentary feeling, and I think it might be hope. It doesn't erase the last seventeen years, Nathan and I still argue and have the occasional fight, it doesn't make up for what a clusterfuck I was as a mother, but maybe there's still time. For something. For some kind of, some shred of redemption.

Thirteen

~~~~~~

Avery

I was the self-appointed premier queer of the Clock School, and that carried with it certain duties and re- sponsibilities, all of which I took both seriously and not seriously. I was a kind of social arbiter. I knew nearly everybody, had been there forever, and I paid attention to social and fashion trends. Who was going out with whom, what people were wearing, who was palling around or not palling around with whom, and I generally knew why.

In short, I paid close and careful attention.

By the end of September, certain things had settled down and trends had been spotted. Nothing dramatic, because how dramatic can it get with a school of a hundred-odd kids? But the leaves were changing on the trees outside; we were noticing the beginning of light coats, pants and shirts re- placing shorts and the lone T-shirt, and we were noticing more boots and shoes intermixed with the standard sneakers and sandals.

Sierra, our fashion leader, was still tall and beautiful, but now had the left side of her head shaved; the remaining hair was streaked black and blond, she had four piercings in each ear, one in a nostril, and she was favoring black, a good deal of leather, and very high heels, which caused her to wobble. She and Anna were still tight, but not as much as last year, and that had everything to do with our most interesting and dramatic new student, Samantha Vash.

Rumor had it that Samantha had spent the previous year in a series of high-class mental hospitals, but you couldn't tell, not as far as I could see. She was the Princess, to my mind. Quite tall, gorgeous, tightly curled light brown hair which she wore in a variety of weaves and plaits, with combs, and sometimes just free and floating like a lovely cloud around her head.

Her clothes were understated and elegant, and her body was long, her carriage erect, and she had shoulders, not insubstantial breasts, and as far as one could discern, the longest legs, and the highest, sweetest, tightest ass I had ever seen. It was a bum that would make a boy proud.

Anna had befriended Samantha. (And as a side note, I did not approve of her nickname, which was Sam. That would be like calling Jacqueline, Jack. Shouldn't she be

Sammy?) And that didn't sit well with Sierra, who had been undisputed Princess for perhaps too long.

Was there room in the Clock School for two Princesses?

Frankly, I thought Sierra pushed her fashion thing a bit far. Tried too hard. As though she was drawing too much attention when she didn't need to. During her hippie stage last year, she wore peasant blouses without a bra for weeks, and had all the straight boys mooing. I couldn't help but think, Dairy products.

The thing is, Sierra is quite bright and funny and interesting, and she doesn't have to go to such lengths. Sierra could walk into a room in jeans and a T-shirt, and you'd notice.

The other thing that caused a stir was that Samantha Vash and Levon Grady, our uncrowned Prince and man of mystery, were engaged together in a major, secret senior project that counted for two courses, and they met alone with Meg in Meg's office for two two-hour sessions a week. With the door closed. And the Clock School is not a closed-door kind of place. Its motto could be All Doors Are Open.

I had known Levon Grady at least half my life, and have had half a crush on him for half that time, like at least half the girls and every queer boy in school. And now this new Princess had arrived, a girl with exquisite taste, with the deportment of a DuPont, and they seemed to have been given special access to each other somehow.

Not that they were necessarily palling around, but they occasionally walked the halls together, and I would see Samantha, Anna, and Levon sitting at the table out back, and that was unusual. Levon at the table, drinking coffee.

He seemed somehow looser, more likely to look up and smile, to say hello, and I had actually had two brief talks with him, one of which he initiated. It was little more than, How're things, Avery? But that was not the sort of thing Levon did. I also once saw him walking with Anna and they were talking and laughing, and that was another thing you did not see.

Louis, my sometime companion and fellow observer, said that Levon was coming out of his shell, but I didn't think so. Asperger kids, no matter where they are on the spectrum, don't come out of their shells, but Louis, like a lot of the kids here, thought those labels, those diagnoses, were—well, to put it bluntly—bullshit. He thought they were diagnoses we were given very early on, and that we molded our behavior to fit the diagnosis.

I partly agreed, but what did I know? When you wash your hands fifty times a day, you've got something wrong with you. Or for that matter, if you're one of the robotics kids, and you wear tie-dye T-shirts every day, there's something wrong with you too. One may be a problem of medicine, one of style. But why can't we tolerate differences? Isn't that the real question?

The coolest girl, and the one who most intrigued me, was Anna. Part of the reason was that she didn't know it. If I liked girls in that way, she'd be the one I'd want. She was kind of on the short side and she was more cute than beautiful. She wore glasses, and had the loveliest pale skin in the world. Her hair was kind of wavy and bobbed at the same time and was reddish brown. She played the trumpet, she went over to the regular high school to take calculus and AP physics, and she organized this Rock the Arts festival every spring where she got all the kids in the high schools to play music, show artwork, do a poetry slam— and tons of kids showed.

She was also a very good writer, as I could attest from being in two writing seminars with her. Clear and brave and honest. (Levon, when he showed his work, could be a brilliant writer as well, but he rarely showed it to anyone but Meg. I wondered if Samantha was now seeing it. And if that could be part of why he might possibly be acting a little differently. If that had anything to do with the mysterious project they were working on.)

The difference between Anna and Sierra was coolness itself, and working at being cool. I guess the word would be *authenticity*.

I need to discuss this with Louis.

Anyway, I'll report back later as things develop. My early-decision application for NYU is nearly done (absurdly early,

I know), but there is just nowhere else for me. Maybe I'll apply to Pratt as a safety school. Whatever happens, a year from now, yours truly will be observing and reporting from the only place really worth reporting and observing from: Lower Manhattan.

I hope the City will be ready.

Fourteen

Levon

I didn't know anybody who didn't know who his dad was.
I knew plenty of kids whose parents were divorced, and
sometimes the dad moved to Colorado or Oregon, but the
kid spent Christmas or Thanksgiving or spring break or
part of the summer with the dad.

Moms always got custody of the kid or kids. Or that's
the way it seemed. Or sometimes one of the parents had
died young, but there were pictures and stories, and aunts
and uncles and cousins and grandparents, and in that way,
the kid kind of got to know the missing parent.

And I suppose in the world there were tons of kids who
didn't know who their fathers were. Say, if your mom was
a prostitute, or the dad just took off when the kid was a baby,
and the mom didn't want to talk about the bum, except to
say he was a bum and a loser and a deadbeat.

But for me, it was like nothing and nobody I knew of. My

mom knew, she just wouldn't tell me. It was always, He doesn't exist. It's best that you not know. It could only harm you.

And I guess I kind of bought that. Susan was so strong and smart and confident. Her whole family was like that. All those doctors, and this is this, and that is that, and you don't question science. And I always got the feeling that they didn't know who he was either. And if Dr. Grady, Susan's father, didn't know, who was I to press the matter?

There were times when I'd bring it up, every once in a great while.

Was he handsome? I'd ask, and Susan would say, Who? And I'd say, My dad.

Forget it, she'd say in this really cold way, and she had this very icy, dismissive manner about her, like a professor whose student had just asked the dumbest question that had ever been known to humankind.

So I learned not to ask. In some way, I learned, at least consciously, not even to think of it. At least almost all the time.

And in my head the question became not, who is my dad, but, why does Susan think it's best for me not to know? What harm would come from knowing?

Then I'd start doing the math, and I'd figure that I had to have been conceived during her last year of grad school.

And so I was probably conceived in Chicago, unless, of course, Susan was away on a trip.

Then I'd think that she was doing all this work with psycho killers in grad school, meeting with them, interviewing them, doing brain scans and such, and that maybe she fell in love with one of them, or felt sorry for one of them, and in some moment, some weak moment of pity or something, she had sex with one and got pregnant. And of course she wouldn't want me to know about that. Having a father who raped and killed a half dozen women, or killed his family, or did some awful, horrible thing.

And I could handle that. I could see feeling pity for someone who was going to live their entire life in a cage. It would be strange as hell, of course, but I could deal.

Otherwise, what the fuck?

It was like you're a very small child, and you imagine creatures under the bed, in the dark, at night. Nothing in reality could be a fraction as bad as what you imagined.

I started imagining everything. A guy who killed and raped twenty-seven women. A guy who killed and ate little children. Someone who burned down a houseful of nuns or unwed mothers, killing all of them.

Or then I thought maybe it was someone I knew. Someone who lived in Ithaca, who taught at Cornell, but was just very strange, or someone who was so ordinary that Susan couldn't admit ever having sex with him. I'd see guys in the street, tall guys in their forties or fifties, with curly hair, and I'd think, That's my father.

And because of her big brain, and her vast knowledge of the brain, and me, and the guy who was my dad, she decided I was unable to handle the knowledge of his existence. Which was worse, I think, than knowing he was dead. Because if he was dead, then I could cry and mourn and go through the stages of grief, and then just get on with life.

But as it was, I had Mom's word, and this gigantic question mark that was dangling there.

Fifteen

~~~~~~~~~~

Susan

I grew up in what was considered a nice *suburb of Kansas* City, Kansas, where oaks and ashes and hemlocks and maples and sycamores had been planted by the city, because fifty miles west of there, there were no trees. Just grasses. Oceans and waves of grasses. Amber waves of grain.

My mother taught high school biology, and my father taught pathology at the University of Kansas Medical School, which was in Kansas City, Kansas, not Lawrence, where the main university campus was. The Jayhawks. Famous for their great basketball teams, where Wilt Chamberlain played way back in the 1950s.

My father taught gross anatomy, but his specialty was forensic anatomy, which had to do with the legal ramifications of anatomy, often in criminal cases, and he frequently taught classes at the Kansas Bureau of Investigation and was consulted on specific cases and often testified in court.

My brothers, Chris and Rob, and I are all tall and blond and straightforward. From birth, it seemed, we were all going into some sort of medicine or science, and Rob and Chris, who make decisions quickly and confidently, became— what else?—general surgeons. But I was a girl, a tall girl, a half inch under five ten, had blond hair, and was—so I was told and so I believe—unusually attractive. But my parents drummed it into me that I was never to slouch, to be in any way ashamed of my height, and that I was bright, and that I was never to play the ditzy, dumb blonde, or to defer to boys in classes, or to hide my light under a bushel.

You don't have to be rude or arrogant, my father said. In fact, you have the extra burden of being kind to those less naturally gifted than yourself. But don't ever be ashamed of your brains, your talent, or your height.

We used to joke as kids that it was a good thing Dad worked with dead people because his bedside manner would have been less than desirable. When we were young, whenever one of us fell and scraped a knee or elbow and started screaming and crying, he would stand us up, and say calmly but firmly, Stop that now. Crying makes you hyperventilate and increases the pain. That's why they teach Lamaze to women in labor. Stop crying. Take slow, deep breaths. Slow, deep, slow, deep. He'd repeat this, and I swear, it worked. The sting didn't go away, but it became something you could manage, you could reason with.

Then he'd take us to the bathroom, wash the scrape off, put on an antiseptic, and bandage the cut or scrape.

But even Mom, who'd grown up tough on a farm, who'd seen the heads of chickens cut off and hogs butchered, sometimes thought Dad could be a bit stringent. We were, she reminded him, children, not cadavers.

One summer, when I was eleven or twelve, I got Dad to take me to the anatomy labs at the medical school. School was not in session, of course, and there were no cadavers present. But I was fascinated by the giant silver lights, the rows of silver beds, which were sloped and had two drains at the base, the hoses, and the trays of shiny tools. Straight and curved scalpels, probes, tweezers, very thin scissors, and something with a handle and a U at the end of it. They seemed almost holy, like the instruments for some sacred rite.

He showed me the wall of silver boxes, and opened one, and pulled it out. It was a long tray or gurney.

This is the cooler, where we keep the bodies. Because the moment life ends, decomposition begins. Cooling the body slows decomposition.

The room smelled funny. It smelled like heavy cleaning fluids, but like other things too. I later learned it was formalin, one of the major tissue preservatives, which seemed to have crept into the very tiles of the room.

So I grew up in a family that was frank, where death and

basic biology were familiar, and where we were all quite comfortable and easy with the very basic things in life. While others squirmed dissecting a frog in high school biology, I went right to it. I was fascinated. It was amazing to me. To see what was inside. I mean, the frog was dead. It didn't feel anything. It was up to us to look and see and discover.

I was also, like my father, fascinated by crime. I believe I read all of *In Cold Blood* in a single weekend when I was thirteen, and I was mesmerized. Not just that it was so vividly written, or that it took place in Kansas, far to the southwest, in Holcomb, but that it got so deeply into the lives and minds of the killers and the killed. Plus it featured the KBI, whom my father often consulted with and taught.

The '70s and '80s were really the golden age of serial killers, if you can call it that. Or more accurately, that's when the public became aware on a grand scale that such people existed. There had been Richard Speck, who killed eight student nurses in 1966 in Chicago, but that was a mass murder, a very different thing from serial murder. Then Charlie Manson, of course, who's hard to characterize—but I think it was Ted Bundy who really put the whole issue, the phenomenon, on the map. Blond, blue-eyed, handsome, articulate, a former law student who had even worked as a counselor on a crisis call line. And he seemed to kill beautiful college-age women with long, often blond, hair. And he was prolific.

Then there was the Zodiac Killer, the Night Stalker, Randy Kraft, the Green River Killer, and John Wayne Gacy, the Killer Clown, who preyed on teenage boys, killed at least thirty-three, and buried twenty-six of them in the crawl space under his house near Chicago. When he wasn't killing, he dressed up in a clown outfit and visited sick children in hospitals.

They seemed to be everywhere, in nearly every state, and it wasn't so much what they did that fascinated me, but why they did it. And the why went beyond the generally bad childhoods, the depravity, the homicidal need for control, all the way to what was going on with their brains. In the neurochemistry and wiring of their brains.

Many millions of people have unspeakably horrible childhoods. Very few become serial murderers.

I graduated second in my high school class, went to the University of Chicago, the place, they said, *where fun goes to die*. Not so for me. I had a blast. I double-majored in biology and chemistry, and did a minor in psychology, just to cover my tracks. I found the psychology, to be perfectly honest, a little bit squishy. A patient tells the shrink, I feel dumb and stupid and ugly. To which the shrink replies, How does that make you feel?

Duh?

I know. I know. Maybe it's important for the patient to articulate his or her feelings, to explore those feelings, their origin, et cetera. But it didn't exactly feel cutting-edge.

In chemistry and biology we were really getting in there. Helping the med students with autopsies, learning about brain chemistry—dopamine, norepinephrine, cortisol, serotonin, beta-blockers, and the extraordinary wiring, the synapses, the electricity of the brain.

I remember an anatomy professor holding up a human brain in his latex-gloved hand, and saying, This, ladies and gentlemen, is far and away the most fabulous, mysterious, complex, beautiful creation on earth and in human history. It has made the music of Bach and the horror of Auschwitz. It makes the most complex supercomputers in the world look like Lincoln Logs.

We had learned more about the brain in the last twenty years than we had in all of human history. About depression, autism and Asperger's, and ADD, about bipolar disorders, and we were coming out of the dark ages. Just fifty years ago they were tapping what amounted to silver ice picks under the upper eyelids of the unmanageably mentally ill, into the frontal lobes of the brains, moving the pick around a little, and calling it therapy. These were prefrontal lobotomies, and tens of thousands of them had turned people into cognitive zombies.

Now we had CAT scans and PET scans and MRIs.

So when I graduated, summa, I went directly into the

Ph.D. program at Chicago. And I began work on MAO-A and MAO-B, otherwise known as the Warrior Gene. It involves the usual feel-good chemicals the brain naturally produces—norepinephrine, epinephrine or adrenaline, serotonin, and dopamine. But it is inhibited in the brain by several other naturally occurring chemicals, notably clorgyline and befloxatone. And we began to find unusually high rates of the MAO-A factor in certain populations, particularly violent criminals. At one point the Warrior Gene was used as a defense in a murder trial. The man was convicted.

It opened whole new worlds of possibility, beyond "my brutal childhood," in trying to understand violence and criminality. But we also found that fighter pilots and top-flight surgeons—neurosurgeons, surgeons who operated on the hearts of one-pound premature babies—had some of these same qualities. A very high tolerance for stress, nerves, you might say, of steel.

I got pregnant in the middle of my last semester. But I was determined to raise the baby alone, and after the move to Ithaca, I taught that first semester, while the baby grew larger and larger in my uterus, and he was born in December. He was nearly nine pounds and twenty-two inches long. And he was very quiet.

He was not an especially cuddly baby. As I suppose, to be honest, I'm not the most cuddly woman. He allowed himself to be held, and he sometimes fell asleep on my chest, but I did not breast-feed him, because I was in my lab so much, though I didn't teach that spring.

But it was his silence that surprised me. He slept through the night from the beginning. He slept long and deep, and he did not make what everyone calls those bright bubbles of sound. I read to him from the beginning—he was always bringing me books to read to him, but he rarely wanted to sit in my lap when we read. He sat next to me, his body pressed against mine, his head bent over, almost blocking the page.

He liked to play alone, or sometimes with one other child, if he could direct the construction of some Lego castle, or some structure made of blocks.

His pediatrician, a gentle Indian man who had been trained in Delhi, said not to worry about the talking, because his hearing was fine, his cognitive functions seemed fine. But the people at Cornell Day Care were all over it. They talked autism, Asperger's, developmentally disabled, they wanted to test him for this and that and some other things too. I refused.

Then suddenly, shortly after his third birthday, in the kitchen, he said, Could I please have a glass of juice, Mother?

It was as though the cat had spoken.

You want that in a sippy cup? I asked.

A regular glass would be fine, he said.

And he began to read books on his own. And not just picture books. Maybe a few to begin with, but by five or six, I remember clearly, he was reading Harry Potter, the first volume, because he would ask me if magic was real or only make-believe.

Make-believe, but you go along with it for the sake of the story.

So Levon was not normal or average. But he was certainly not disabled.

Sixteen

~~~~~~~~~~

Anna

By mid- to late October, Sam and I were hanging out a fair bit. It's not like we were close-close. In some ways, I don't think anybody got real close to Sam, maybe because of the year in the hospital, or whatever her disorder was, though as the years passed I was beginning to believe less and less in the so-called disorders of the kids at the Clock School. I mean, everybody at our age was a little depressed and pretty anxious and kind of Aspergery and a little ADD. It kind of sucked being a teenager, just as I heard my grandfather say it sucked getting old. Your bones ached, and you couldn't pee straight or sleep very well, and it just came with the age. Being a teenager was like that. You just had to go through it.

But Sam and I would take off between classes and get a coffee at Gimme! She loved the double cappuccino where they made the beautiful leaf pattern on top, and I loved the double espresso, which felt like doing cocaine, even though I'd only tried cocaine once at a party and couldn't stop sneezing.

Then we'd go over to Triangle Park, or sometimes drive to Stewart Park at the south end of Cayuga Lake. We'd grab a bench, or if it was warm, sit on the grass in the sun.

She'd ask how it was all going, 'cause I had this thing for Noah Law, a kid who was in my AP physics class, and I'd laugh and say, Real, real slow. I'd say, You got any suggestions?

She'd say, Me? That's like asking the mouse how to catch the cat.

You don't like boys?

She picked a blade of grass, blew it to the wind, then looked over the expanse of lake and hills.

Lemme put it this way. Between hospitals, and my crazy mother, and depression, I've had about a half dozen dates, and they were usually with half-drunk boys trying to grab my boobs, and it was all pretty limited. They had all the charm and conversation of a dog trying to sniff your crotch.

I started laughing.

Charming, I said.

Anyone here interest you? I asked.

Well, there is Levon, but Levon is kind of wonderful and impossible. You know that better than me.

I nodded. Yeah, I said. I don't know him much, but he really does seem like the man of mystery and intrigue.

We were quiet.

How's that project with him?

Well, I'm not allowed to divulge any secrets, but we're supposed to be kind of writing our life histories. And maybe interviewing other people about ourselves, or having them write what they know of us, and stuff. And we're writing our own memories and histories and such.

Some ducks moved by in the water, and a bunch of seagulls were squawking overhead. People walked and jogged on the Waterfront Trail, and now and then a car would pass slowly by on the road that snaked through the park.

That sounds pretty interesting. Pretty intense.

It is. Way more than I thought it would be. But Meg swore us to secrecy. Only Levon, Meg, and I can see what we write, and what's written.

Damn.

And I'm not trying to be coy or proprietary or anything. It gets really personal, and kind of traumatic, and we just couldn't do it if half the school knew what we were writing about.

No, I totally understand.

We each sipped, and I said, I wonder how Meg paired

you two. Levon's been here forever, and you were completely new.

I dunno. All she said when we met in the summer and she'd read this long file on me was that she thought we might work well together. She also said it could be a disaster, but she said if we both agreed, she thought it would have a good chance of working. She even said—and these are her words—it might be *brilliant*.

Is it?

I don't know from brilliant, but so far so good.

When we were done with our coffee and were getting in Sam's car, Sam suddenly asked, You hungry?

Kinda.

You wanna stop at my house for lunch? It's just up the hill. Five minutes.

You sure?

Yeah. You'd be doing me a huge favor. I've never brought a friend home, and if my weird mom's there, it would get her off my back. She's always asking me if I'm making friends. You'd be my sacrificial lamb. And my dad could be there, and he's a sweetie. It would be huge to me, and I'm so damn nervous about bringing someone home. We can grab food and eat in the garden. And that's worth seeing. Some horticulture professor used to own the house. It's a great garden.

Sure. Let's do it. People always tell me I have good social skills.

You have excellent social skills. Very good manners. Like you balanced books on your head while walking at finishing school.

Yes, I said. In France, then Switzerland. And learned the proper way to serve tea and cucumber sandwiches.

We drove up the steep hill above I-High, then went on Cayuga Heights Road, which is pretty fancy. Big houses, set way back from the road. This was where the doctors and lawyers and emeritus professors lived. She took a right off Cayuga Heights Road, and three or four houses up, on this really sweet street, with very big old trees, she pulled into a driveway with a fairly big front yard that had an enormous beech tree, with that smooth silver bark and the almost purple leaves.

The house was like an oversize bungalow, I think they're called. Kind of English and kind of Arts and Crafts, if I knew what I was talking about. My mom was interested in houses. It had these long overhanging eaves, and porches on the first and second floors, and it was dark green, so it kind of blended into the landscape, but it had orange shutters like Halloween. From the outside, at least, it looked kind of amazing. There was also a big garage at the back of the driveway, which looked like it must have been a carriage house. There were outside steps leading to the upper story, and curtains in the windows up there.

An Accord and a red Mini Cooper were parked in front of the garage.

We stopped, and Sam said, Thanks for this, and I said, C'mon, it's nothing.

We went in a side door, and the place was nice. Really nice. Marble counters, and a checked tile floor in the kitchen, and Sam called, Mom, and this woman with blond hair came in, and she was a looker. She wore those round black glasses that schoolmarms wore in the 1930s, but had become cool again, and leather boots that came almost to her knees, and jeans, and this really nice black sweater that must have been cashmere.

This is Anna, Sam said. And this is my mom.

Vera, her mom said, and she stepped forward, and she smiled, and she shook my hand, then she gave me a hug, as though she was grateful Sam had a friend.

We came to get some lunch, Sam said, and I said, Nice to meet you.

I can make sandwiches, order in, anything, Vera said, and she looked suddenly nervous.

No, no. We'll just grab a yogurt, a banana, an apple. Then maybe sit in the garden, Sam said.

Then there was a tall man in jeans and a fairly rumpled sweater behind Vera. One shirttail in front was untucked.

Hey, Dad. This is Anna. My friend from school.

Hi, Anna from school, he said, and smiled. He seemed way more relaxed. His hair was kind of wavy and had little streaks of gray, and wasn't combed.

Honey, Vera said, you look like you just rolled out of bed.

But I am rolling, he said, and patted her hip.

Can I see the house? I said. If that isn't rude. It's so beautiful.

Sure, her dad said. And please call me Nathan.

He had rimless glasses, and he led the way. The floors were polished hardwood, and the windows were leaded, and it was bigger inside than it looked from the outside. The furniture in the dining room was new, Swedish or something, and older in the big living room, which had a fireplace, and couches, and nooks with chairs, and a big bay window that looked out onto the garden, which was amazing. There was a window seat, and a den that was all windows and had tons of books and CDs, and a telescope in one window.

There were flowers in vases and art on the walls, and the light fell on Persian rugs that looked like they came from Persia. Rich scarlet and gold and blue patterns that were just beautiful.

We can skip the second floor, Nathan said, but maybe Sam can show you her aerie.

The two of us hustled up the stairs, which were gleaming, came to a big landing, then up another set of stairs to the third floor. There were three doors, and the floors were beautiful. There was one small bedroom, a bathroom, and then a big bedroom under the eaves with slanted ceilings, three leaded windows at the end, a queen-size bed, a couch, two big chairs, a desk, two closets, and all the usual girl stuff. It felt beautiful and private.

God, I said. This is all yours.

Sam nodded.

Lucky girl. This is seriously cool. But there's nothing on the walls.

She nodded again.

How come?

I haven't quite moved in yet.

I nodded. There was a certain sadness when she said that.

You will, I said.

Hope so.

I bounced on the bed.

I wish my mom wouldn't wear those boots, she said. She thinks it makes her look twenty-two.

Oh, they're okay, I said.

Sam shook her head.

My mom can be so lame, can try so hard to be cool, when that's the last thing she is.

I was surprised at her sudden vehemence.

Well, anyway. Shall we get something to eat? she asked.

Sure.

Downstairs, Vera had put yogurts and bananas and apples and cloth napkins on a tray for us. She had also set out brownies and glasses of milk.

You might want to eat in the garden, she said, and Sam said, Thanks, Mom.

So we sat outside, at this glass table, on these really comfortable chairs, and the garden, even in the fall, was something. These curves, and terraces, and a scarlet maple, and fall flowers, and you felt you were in a little piece of Eden.

I didn't exactly grow up in a trailer, but you could feel the money here. Not showy, but these people had it. And I wondered how that changed a person. If it made you entitled or guilty or more secure.

This is beautiful, I said.

I like this house, Sam said. In Boston, we lived in this three-million-dollar museum place with a cook and nanny. It was disgusting. I swear. It ate your soul. It really fucked us up.

Well, welcome to the regular world.

We ate a yogurt, I had a banana, she ate an apple. We sipped milk, and then we thought we should get rolling.

We brought the tray in, thanked Vera and Nathan, and Vera said, Please come again. It was so nice to see you.

In the car, Sam said, almost crying, You don't realize what a favor you just did me.

Sweetie, I said. It was fun. I enjoyed it.

Really, she said, and by then she was shaking, she was trembling. You're the first friend to come to my house in . . . like . . . six, seven years.

Pull over, I said.

She did, and I said, Come here. I hugged her, and she held on, and I could feel her shaking. And we must have stayed like that for three or four minutes. I said, I don't know anyone who's not mortified by their parents.

Okay, she said. I survived. You still like me?

A ton, I said. More than ever.

Seventeen

〜〜〜

Carrie

I was the social worker at Fall Creek School for fourteen years, after my husband and kids and I moved here from Ann Arbor, Michigan, nearly twenty-two years ago. He set up practice in urology, and our three were in middle and high schools then, and I didn't want to stay home watching *Oprah* and doing craft projects. Not that there was anything wrong with that, if that lit you up, but I liked schools and kids, and making my tiny, nearly invisible mark in the world.

And Fall Creek was perfect in so many ways. We lived just up the hill from it, in the lower part of Cayuga Heights. It had a wonderful range of students, from faculty brats to the children of single mothers on welfare, and it was smaller than any of the other primary schools in the city, I believe. It seemed right-sized, nice-sized, and I really, really liked a lot of the teachers who had been there awhile and who were remarkably gifted and energetic and talented. Not all of them, of course, but an unusually high percentage.

I believe it was Emily Ford, his second-grade teacher, who first brought Levon Grady to my attention. She stopped in my office after school—this would have been about ten years ago—and she said she had the most extraordinary boy in her class, with an almost equally remarkable mother. I remember she joked, You got time? And when I said, Sure, she said, Three hours?

She told me about Levon. Tall, exceptionally bright, off the charts in all his tests, quite handsome, socially maladroit, but not clumsy, in fact, very graceful, and that was significant, because Asperger's spectrum kids are often physically awkward. But a deep loner, only she didn't know where the loneliness was coming from. Social or biological.

So, she calls the mother in, Susan Grady, professor of neurobiology at Cornell, who is also quite tall and very striking, and she wants to know what the problem is. Not warm or friendly. Great kid, perfect academically, but socially isolated.

Not surprised, Professor Grady said. His father was quite firmly on the Asperger's scale.

That doesn't mean Levon is.

Miss Ford, she said, as though looking at a spot on the wall, I am a neurobiologist. This is my field of expertise.

Sometimes, I said to her, we get the results we expect before the experiment is finished.

I'm aware of that predilection, but I know my boy and I know my science.

Have you ever considered that he might be lonely? I asked.

I have, and I'm quite certain that he's not.

Would you object, Emily Ford said, if Levon were to meet with the school social worker?

Susan Grady smiled. Of course not, she said. Why should I?

Then, Emily said, she fairly fled the room in a gust of wind, skirts and scarves flying.

I first met Levon a week or so later, after lunch but before gym class, and I said, I'm Carrie Miller. I'm the school social worker, but I suspect you know what I do.

He stood looking at a Japanese mask on the windowsill and a silk Japanese print on the wall. My husband and I had spent a year in Japan when our children were very young.

Yes. You talk and help people with their problems, problems of social adjustment, and stuff like that. And you like Japan. Or Japanese things.

I love the country, and the things.

There was a Bashō haiku engraved on a tile:

A flash of lightning:
Into the gloom
Goes the heron's cry.

That's beautiful. What is it?

A Japanese poem called a haiku. Very short. This one is by Bashō, perhaps their greatest master of haiku. It's not only a poem, but it kind of makes you pause. Creates stillness. There's a tiny contradiction in it. The lightning, the disappearance of the heron's cry into the gloom. The cry and the lightning, how they become one. It stills the mind.

He said it out loud:

A flash of lightning:
Into the gloom
Goes the heron's cry.

Very beautiful, he said.

Please sit down, I said. And he did, and this would be the first of many remarkable hours I spent with this remarkable boy. We met every other week for nearly three and a half years, and my gosh, what didn't we talk about?

We talked about books and movies and video games. We talked about the wars in the Middle East, about his teachers, and why he liked some, and didn't like others. Mrs. Vara in fourth grade treated them like they were in first grade and was overcontrolling, but Mrs. O'Mara and Mrs. Mangino, who shared the two third-grade classes, were funny and really creative and always made things new and interesting. They were confident about themselves as teachers, and that made everything go well. And Emily Ford, who introduced us, Ms. Ford was one of the coolest. She ran marathons, and she could jump from a standing position to the top of a desk, just like that. She'd do it when she felt they weren't paying attention or were getting sleepy-headed.

Levon didn't have many or any friends, but he taught Dylan, a very unpopular boy from a very sad, very broken home, to play chess, and then when he saw Keesha, another sad kid from another sad family, watching, he taught her too. Sometimes he ate lunch with them because he didn't want them to eat by themselves, and when he saw other kids picking on them in the hallways or starting to bully them on the playground or in the gym, he always tried to defend them.

Despite the fact that he himself was friendless, he was respected. He was very bright, and he was a big kid, and at kickball he could kick the ball out of the playground onto the street, and during fitness week each year, he did more pull-ups than anyone.

The kid clearly had empathy, even deep empathy, and that was not something you saw in Asperger's. So despite my better judgment, I requested an appointment with Susan Grady, I believe when Levon was in fourth grade, and we had been talking for over a year. I had grown enormously fond of him.

She came in, and she was impressive-looking, though one was not impressed by her humility. I had googled her, and was aware of her credentials, her work in neuroscience, and the fact that she'd been made full professor in her early thirties.

We shook hands, sat down, and she said, So you're Carrie Miller, who I've been hearing such glowing reports of.

Really, I said, and felt myself blushing.

Levon is quite fond of you, and extremely fond of your talks. He very much looks forward to them.

I'm so pleased to hear that. He's quite the boy. Utterly remarkable in every way.

I think so, she said.

She looked at the Japanese mask, at the tile with the Bashō.

You've spent time in Japan?

My husband and children and I spent a year there years ago; it was part of his post-residency training in urology.

Interesting. My father was a doctor too. A pathologist.

Doctor brats, eh.

She smiled.

Might I ask what you wanted to see me for?

To talk about Levon.

Specifically.

I find Levon to be all the usual things we say about him. Very bright, handsome, kind, thoughtful, but also quite isolated. He's, as far as I can see, virtually friendless.

I'm aware of that, Susan said.

Which would indicate the possibility of his being somewhere on the very broad spectrum of Asperger's. The very high-functioning end.

That's possible, but those terms don't mean much to me. You see, his father was a graduate student, whom I had a very brief tryst with at the end of our time at the University of Chicago. He was a brilliant physicist, now a professor in the Midwest. He was probably somewhere in the middle of the spectrum. But he functions quite well within the bubble of a university.

He has never met Levon, she added.

So you think he inherited Asperger's?

I think it's possible.

Susan, if I may, I don't think Levon has Asperger's. In fact, if he were tested, I think he would fail the test.

Why do you say that?

He's deeply empathic. He's physically graceful, extremely so. With me, in our talks, there's nothing but give and take. There's no one-sided verbosity. There's reciprocity. I think his symptoms are learned behavior, not inherited. He's picked up cues from a very early age, and he's very smart, a brilliant student, if you will. I just don't think he's been encouraged to be social.

Are you suggesting that I've encouraged and shaped antisocial behavior?

I think Levon is shy. I think he likes his alone time, far more than others.

I paused before I continued. To be frank, yes. I think parents shape and influence their children profoundly, consciously or unconsciously, for good or bad reasons. I suspect you wanted to protect your son. You didn't want him to be hurt, the way you imagined his father was hurt as a child.

Ms. Miller, I am a neurobiologist. More than that, I know and love my son. I'm sure you mean well, and I'm glad you enjoy your talks with him and his time with you, but I think you're wrong. Wrong that I would deliberately harm Levon.

We often do what we do out of fear, out of the very best of intentions. Would you allow us to test him?

No. Emphatically no.

Would you think about it?

Absolutely not. Testing is unnecessary. I know my son and I know how the brain works.

Her gaze was so commanding, her tone so adamant, it seemed futile to press the issue.

So I suppose you would wish that I no longer meet with him, I said.

Why would I want that? Of course you can meet.

And so we did. Through the end of fifth grade and his graduation from Fall Creek School. A year or two later I retired from the school system entirely. The testing had taken over, the testing of students, of teaching, the teaching to the test. The paperwork got worse and worse, and my kids were off to college by then.

I still think of Levon, and I wonder what will become of him. He will do interesting things in this world. I think of him and his remarkable talent, and I'm reminded of the line from the British novelist E. M. Forster: Only connect.

That, more than anything, is what I wish for Levon.

Eighteen

~~~~~~

Sam

So on Friday, on one of those lovely fall afternoons, with the trees blazing gold and yellow and orange and purple, and the sun shining like it was June or something, Levon and I happened to be leaving school at the same time, and we started walking together.

He was walking home, and I was walking to my car, which I had parked on Lewis Street, about a half block from his house, roughly two blocks from school. We fell in step, and I asked him what he was up to that weekend, and he kind of grunted.

Which for some reason irritated me. I wasn't sure why except that I wouldn't see him for three days, until Monday. I loved being around him, I was starting to realize.

What's ever up? he said.

I mean, what do you do all weekend?

He said he read, and played with computers, and slept, and did what anyone did.

I don't think that's what everyone does, Levon.

Yeah, what does everyone do?

They see their friends, they go out, see movies, go to each other's houses, hang out with other people.

We reached my car, and he kept walking.

Could we talk? I asked him, and he stopped, came back a few steps, and we stood, leaning against the car.

You think maybe I could see you some weekend? I asked.

I'd never have had said such a thing, but he was really irritating me, with his grunt, his lack of response, and I wanted to put him on the spot.

See you? he said.

Like maybe you could come over to my house, or I could come to your house, or we could go out and eat pizza or see a movie or even take a walk. You know. Something slightly normal.

He was staring at his shoes, or at the beautiful leaves on the sidewalk.

I thought we weren't supposed to be normal.

Where's that written? I asked.

Probably in our files.

And that's gospel? We're supposed to live according to what's written in our fucking school files?

No, but—

We didn't say anything for what seemed like ten minutes, but was probably more like twenty seconds.

Can I ask you something else? I said.

I didn't know where my courage came from. Maybe I'd
taken an extra Ambien, but I think I wanted to break through
to something else, some other level.

Sure, he said. And I could tell he was kind of nervous.
Like he wanted to run away.

Do you trust me? I asked.

Trust you?

Yeah. Trust me. Or do you think I'll hurt you or betray
you?

He looked up at the trees and telephone wires and houses.

I trust you. I show you my writing. I've never done that
before.

So how about we spend a little time together outside
school?

But what would we do?

We could maybe take a walk. That's pretty simple.

I'm not sure, he said. When would we do that?

I laughed, despite myself, because it was a serious question for him.

Any time. I could call you, or you could call me. Maybe
some afternoon. Just get out of the house. Try something
different. It won't kill you.

Saturday or Sunday? he asked.

Does it matter?

Maybe. Maybe not.

I took his arm.

I don't want to be pushy, and I don't want to make you uncomfortable, but I like you. I'm interested in spending time with you.

Just then, an old lady with a little white dog on a leash turned the corner from Utica Street and started walking slowly toward us. When she was about ten feet away, she said, Lovely day, and we both said, Yes, and then she passed.

We stood for a while and didn't say anything, and finally Levon said, So maybe this weekend? A walk, or something regular people do.

I'll call, I said.

Or I'll call.

Then I got in the car and started it up, and I watched him walk toward his house. Maybe I should have felt elated and relieved, and I did feel those things. But I was also shaky and scared and such a mixture of things that I wasn't even sure what I was feeling.

Then I got home and lay on top of my bed, and I actually started crying, with happiness and fear, and maybe wondering what in the name of God I had just done.

Nineteen

Meg

The weeks were flying by, and all had been well. Then I don't know what happened. Perhaps things were just going too well, too easily. Too many primroses in the path, rainbows in the sky, rosy sunsets. It was all just dandy, just the way I had hoped and dreamed, and two months in—boom. I got two cats in a bag, and darn, it happened fast. And I'm not sure why, or even when.

In early fall, Sam wrote that incredible piece on Groton. Levon wrote this quite moving account of being alone on a long weekend one fall, when he was six or seven, and his mother was away at a conference up at Cornell pretty much the whole weekend, and he played video games, and fooled around on his computer, and read books. He made himself mac and cheese, and peanut butter and jelly sandwiches, and he didn't see his mother from Friday afternoon until Sunday evening, and he remembered how it rained the entire weekend, and the wind blew, and the leaves were blowing off the trees, stripping the branches, and he just didn't know what he was doing most of the time. What was he supposed to be doing? Why was he there? In that house? On that weekend? On the earth? In time? It all seemed so stupid and useless.

Sam said, quite fairly, I thought that he sounded lonely. That who wouldn't be lonely?

And he said, I'm so fucking sick of that word, *lonely*. I've heard it all my life.

Well, I said, were you?

No, he said.

Sorry, Sam said.

Don't apologize, Levon said. No sorry needed.

Then we were quiet.

Oddly enough, it was November outside, and the trees were losing their leaves, but it had been unusually warm and sunny on the way into school that day.

I mean, he said, isn't it natural and normal to suffer, to feel pain? Isn't that the first of the Four Noble Truths of Buddhism? To live is to suffer?

Sure, I said. But isn't there enough suffering already, without compounding it, making it worse? Sam in the shower at Groton, you home alone an entire rainy weekend when you're six or seven, wondering why you even exist?

Surely it doesn't have to be that bad? Sam said.

But don't you think we make it worse by dwelling on it, picking at the scabs and scars, going over it again and again? Never getting past it? Levon said.

He looked at us, both angry and pleading.

You get knocked down, you pick your sorry ass up, and you move on, he continued.

But sometimes if you never look at it, you revisit it, and repeat it and repeat it, forever and ever, I said.

Didn't Einstein say that insanity was doing the same thing over and over and expecting to get different results, Sam said.

Or Plato, I said: The unexamined life is not worth living.

You can flip those, Levon said: The unlived life is not worth examining. Or, if at first you don't succeed, try, try again.

Or Santayana, I believe, I said: If you forget your history, you're doomed to repeat it.

Again, we had a Quaker Silence.

I'll be honest, Levon said. This would be a lot easier if we didn't have to meet. If we could just write our stuff, and get other people to write, and not meet.

I know what you mean, Sam said.

I felt almost betrayed or attacked suddenly. Like, what had I done? And Sam looked hurt.

Would you rather not meet? I asked her.

No, I like meeting. It's hard, it's pretty uncomfortable

sometimes, but I always feel better afterward, for facing the fear.

Levon? I said.

I find it very uncomfortable. It makes me want to hide under the desk.

Like a little kid? I said.

He smiled. Like a little kid.

You feel exposed?

He nodded.

Frightened?

He kept nodding.

As though we won't think so well of you?

Correct.

How did you feel when you read about Levon on his rainy weekend alone, Sam? I asked.

I wished I could have been there.

And, Levon, when you read about Sam at Groton?

Same thing. I hated her loneliness. I wanted to be there.

Are those not good impulses? Good feelings?

I think they are, in some ways, Sam said. Except they're past. I can't do anything about that weekend.

But you can understand a little of where Levon's been.

I'm not sure he wants me to know. I wish he did, sometimes desperately, but he's got all these walls surrounding him, and I feel shut out, rejected.

Levon?

I like and respect Sam. Isn't that enough? Why do I need to know everything about her?

Maybe you two should think about that. It seems to me we can only move forward. And maybe we started too fast.

When I read Sam's Groton piece, Levon said, I was so moved, and there were so many things I felt and wanted to say, I actually called her at night, at like ten thirty. I texted first, to see if I could call, and she said sure. It took me about five minutes to actually send the text. And she texted back and said, Sure. Call.

So I called, and you know what I said. Because I don't know if I've ever called a girl. I said, I read your Groton piece. It was great. I'm glad you're not dead. Then I hung up.

That's really thoughtful, I said.

I'm glad you're not dead, Levon said. That's the most pathetic piece of praise, of empathy I've ever heard, or ever heard of.

I was mortified afterward, he went on. I thought, You bonehead.

What'd you think? I asked Sam.

I thought it was charming. It was brief, it was very much Levon, and I was really touched and grateful, and kind of shocked that he called. And I also thought it was pretty brave of him to call me. I was really moved.

Levon? I asked.

I'm too embarrassed to respond, he said.

This project was supposed to make everything better, but it didn't. I'm always trying to make everything better. As a shrink once said to me, Meg, why do you think it's your job to manage everybody's feelings?

Sam started to pull back, to write this really bitter, spiteful stuff about her life in Chestnut Hill and her mother. She said that while her father worked twelve- and fourteen-hour days, and made millions, her mother, who had an M.B.A. from Harvard, turned into a professional mommy. Only she wasn't a professional mommy at all because first they had a nurse who lived in one of the two apartments at the back of their huge and tasteful house, and then she had a series of au pairs from either Switzerland or Germany, who were always young and blond and beautiful and spoke nearly flawless English. Plus there was always a black maid, who was from Trinidad or Tobago, and kept everything clean and shiny, and who cooked, and did the laundry, and told stories in heavily accented English about her faraway country where the sun shined all the time and the men fished, and there were palm trees, and the sand was white on the beaches and the sea was very, very blue.

So her mother did what? Was what? She belonged to a country club. She played bridge. She drank cocktails in the afternoon by the pool in the summer, alone, or with her other non-mommy mommy friends, or by the fireplace in the "great room." (They really called it the "great room" because it was enormous and was at the center of the house and had about six couches, and a fireplace big enough to roast a pig in, and a partially glass ceiling far overhead.) They'd have cocktails by the fireplace, and if it started to snow outside, they could look out the windows, onto the small woods outside, or overhead, and watch the flakes swirl down.

She changed clothes several times a day because she had two immense walk-in closets set next to the giant master suite, and she shopped at least twice a week. Every month or two she'd fly to New York City and stay at the Ritz with one or two of her friends. She'd go to a museum, see a show on Broadway, but mostly she shopped. Shoes, coats, dresses, belts, blouses, silky underthings.

And the house itself. Designed by some famous architect in the 1950s, or by the student of some famous architect in the '50s. It was glass and concrete and chrome and steel, and made in a series of interconnected pods, like some space station. There were several floors, two or three, but it was hard to tell. You could get lost, because stairways were everywhere, and half stairways, and small rooms, and huge rooms, and long and short hallways, and many windows.

The rest of it was like being smothered, where you had to be careful how you breathed, of what you thought or said. Because this was ten thousand square feet, and was designed by a famous architect, or his student, and cost

2.8 million dollars, or 3.7 mil, or some huge figure. And most people would kill to live here, said Mom.

When we talked about it together, Levon had little to say. He said it was passionate, and said the life sounded pretty meaningless and empty, but it was pretty far from any life he'd ever known.

It sounds pretty soul-killing, I said. But what about your dad?

He worked and worked. But when he was around, it was always easier.

You think your mom was happy?

God, no. I think she hated herself. Even more than I hated myself.

Why would you hate yourself? Levon asked.

Sam looked at him. She looked and looked.

I don't understand that question, she finally said.

You didn't do anything wrong, he said.

She stared at him, and finally she looked at me, and then she looked at the floor.

I don't know what to say, she finally said.

We sat in our Quaker Silence for several minutes. Finally I said, Maybe we should just end here for today. Think about this.

I stood up and said, Let's bring it in.

Sam said, I don't feel like bringing much in today.

Levon paused, looked at his shoes a moment.

Well, let's do it anyway, Levon said.

So we grabbed each other and hugged, and I noticed that Levon had his head leaning against Sam's head. A good sign?

I didn't know. Perhaps. Perhaps not.

Twenty

~~~~~~~~

Noah

I guess I was one of the robotics kids, but I didn't wear tie-dye shirts. I didn't own one, and I've never understood why they always wore them. I was never exactly a cool dresser, but my dad, who was a lawyer, said that there was once a really funny article in his college alumni magazine called something like, "Why Do Scientists Dress So Badly?" There was a picture of a professor lecturing in front of a whiteboard of equations, and he was wearing a checked suit coat, a striped tie, and, he swears, checkered pants that were two inches too short, and he had a sock on only one foot.

My mother said the picture had to be a setup, stage-managed, but Dad said, No, it was true. Scientists, on the whole, were pretty bad dressers.

Looking cool, for them, was a turtleneck with a corduroy blazer. That was styling in the chemistry department, he said.

Anyway, I was having lunch in the cafeteria, which they pretentiously called the "Café," particularly considering what passed for food in the place. Half an English muffin, covered with ketchup and little sprinkles of American cheese, micro-waved for thirty seconds was called "pizza." "Salad" was a few leaves of wilted lettuce, a cherry tomato, and a few shavings of carrot. I swear, if this were a prison, they'd riot. I usually got a yogurt and an apple or banana because how could you fuck that up?

I usually ate with Avery or Sierra or Anna, sometimes Levon, but that day Sam stopped and said, Mind if I sit with you?

Absolutely, I said. I mean, I absolutely don't mind. Please.

She smiled that dazzling smile, and sat, and she had—what else?—a banana and yogurt. Maybe she felt sorry for me, sitting alone. Maybe it was just Sam being kind. Who knows why she'd want to sit with the likes of me.

How's the food today? she said, smiling.

The best, I said. Top of the line.

We started talking about colleges and SATs, because pretty much all the seniors had taken the SATs and were applying to schools. Everyone was hearing back from the November SAT tests and just about everyone had done quite well, which you kind of expected at this school. Anna was relatively low at just over 2000, and so far Levon—no surprise—was high at 2330, which was kind of ridiculous, and kind of expected.

How'd your SAT go? I asked, and she said, Good.

Can I ask?

2360, she said.

Holy shit, I said. You beat Levon.

He was higher in math, but I was higher in verbal and writing.

My God, you could go to MIT, or Caltech.

Right, she said, laughing.

You know where you're applying?

I think just Cornell and maybe Swarthmore. I just got here, and I don't want to leave. How 'bout you?

Oh, mostly smaller places. Williams, Oberlin, Grinnell, Kenyon, Bates. What about Levon?

I think Cornell and Brown.

Hmmm, I said.

Can I ask you something? Sam said, looking down at the table.

Sure. Anything.

What's up with Levon's father? What's the big mystery?

I was kind of taken aback.

I know as little as you do, I said. Just these crazy rumors. That he might have been one of her mom's study subjects, like some psycho killer back in Chicago, or some mystery man she knew in grad school. Nobody knows. Not even

Levon. And no one even knows why Levon doesn't know except that his mother won't tell him. Which, of course, makes it all the more mysterious.

She kept looking at the table.

That's all pretty strange, she said. It would make me crazy.

We were silent awhile.

I had been kind of crushing on Sam since the start of school, but I sort of knew that wasn't going to happen. For one thing, she was taller than me, and for another, while I got the sense that she liked and respected me in our Quest for Justice class, it was like, not like-like. I could feel something between her and Levon. I didn't know what it was. Like-like. Love-hate. But it was this really strong vibe that was positive and negative, like a magnetic force field.

Avery, who was very sharp about these things, and who had lunch and coffee with both of them, said he could get absolutely nothing directly from either of them. That they locked him completely out. And he said that told him more than anything that something was going on. Not anything romantic, and he was sure there was nothing sexual—yet, he added. He was certain they were both virgins.

But it was something powerful and old and deep, and it had to do with their project with Meg, and how fucked up they had both been. He said they were both so volatile. Especially Levon. Sam was better at hiding it than Levon, and he was sure it wasn't med changes, or stuff at either of their homes. It was like alchemy, and he was dying to find out.

My lunch with Sam ended with us eating in silence, and when I told Avery about it after school, he grilled me until he had every last detail about Sam's interest in Levon.

This is my quest, he said. To figure them out. Without intruding, of course. He smiled. That, and NYU.

Then he said, What about you and Anna?

He'd been pushing me to ask Anna out for coffee. He said we were both cool, and she didn't know me, and if she knew me even a little more, she'd like me a lot more.

We have lunch, I said.

At which you ask a lot of questions, and she rattles on, he said.

He was right.

Honey, he said, and he put his hand on mine. Take it from me. You're a looker, a catch, and a very interesting young man.

With OCD.

Oh, please. Who gives a shit if you wash your hands a lot, and take too many showers.

Avery.

Noah. My friend. I'm not saying get over it. I'm saying just do it anyway. Courage, as we know, is not the absence of fear, but acting despite the fear.

It's funny, but as I looked across the table at him, I realized I'd been friends with Avery for more than twelve years. Even though he was funny, and vamped it up, and was the biggest gossip in Ithaca, he was also one of the most thoughtful, decent friends I'd ever had. And he always had been. He never pretended to be anything he wasn't.

Sitting there, I suddenly felt this sharp pang, almost of sweet anguish—that we only had a few more months of our childhood in Ithaca together.

Okay, I said.

Okay what?

I'll ask Anna for coffee. We'll get double caps and sit in Triangle Park.

That's my tiger, he said. That's my big boy.

Then he smiled and said, So what's the news. What do you hear? Anything new going on?

I shook my head. You're relentless, I said.

He looked around the Café. The news never rests, he said.

Twenty-one

~~~~~~~

Trevor

When I came to the University of Chicago in 1991, I came with the intention of pursuing an advanced degree in mathematics, in number theory, to be more precise. I had received my bachelor's degree at the University of Manchester in the United Kingdom, and I was very much interested indeed in prime numbers, in pattern recognition, integers, and in the more useless and, if I may say so, elegant and even beautiful work of higher mathematics.

I began to work with Dr. Frank Liu, who was in both higher mathematics and physics, and who at the time was beginning to explore the field of light. Was it a wave or a particle? It is both, of course, but he was applying certain theories of mathematics, of laws of motion and probability distributions and lenses and lasers, and coming up with some startling results.

Light is very strange, and mysterious, and a paradox. Most

scientists had believed that light was a simple wave that went from point A to point B. They found that light was made of very tiny waves, very short ultraviolet waves of light to slightly longer waves on the spectrum that were red. But in the early twentieth century physicists began to examine that. In a famous experiment they shined light through two slots in a metal wall, like two doorways. They found that the light passed through the doors as a wave, but it emerged on the other side as a particle. This doesn't sound like much, but it was an extraordinary revolution in physics. It was essentially the beginning of quantum mechanics, and it has been a paradox and mystery to physicists ever since. How could something like light be both smooth, flowing waves at times, and at other times gritty particles. It was and is something no scientist really, fully understands.

Dr. Liu is a brilliant and charming man, and within one year under his tutelage, I was a graduate student in physics, with a special interest in light.

I am not a normal person and have never been one, since the time of my early childhood. I am physically awkward, have limited social skills, and do not even like to make eye contact with those to whom I am speaking. I test very high in many academic areas and was always a top student, if I was left alone.

What people don't know is that I grew up as the youngest

son of a tenant farmer in a very remote part of East Anglia in England, and that we were desperately poor. I was the youngest of four by some margin; the next oldest was seven years older than I. Everyone worked extremely hard, and we had no electricity, nor did we have indoor plumbing until our family left the farm for factory work in a small town some twenty or thirty kilometers distant. I was alone virtually all of the first seven years of my life.

In fact, I dislike being touched, and I often feel intensely uncomfortable around other people, except in very specific conditions. Which is to say, do not expect me to be like a regular person. I am simply not one.

Which leads me to the point at hand: Susan Grady, who was a graduate student in neurobiology at the same time I was a graduate student in physics at Chicago. We finished the same year. In fact, we had seen each other around the science quads for five years, and I was very much aware of her. Who would not be?

She was five feet ten inches tall, had red-brown hair, which she often wore piled on top of her head, was quite attractive, and also stood and walked with squared shoulders; she did not slouch the way so many tall women do, as though their height was something about which to be embarrassed. She was famous among graduate students in the sciences because she was studying the MAO-A gene, the so-called Psychopath Gene. She was studying PET and

CAT scans of the brains of violent criminals, and she was considered a star.

She was also quite friendly, and she always made a point of saying, Hello, Trevor, in a bad English accent, when we passed.

She must have heard a thing or two about me, because I was working with Dr. Liu, and I am not entirely unattractive, despite my considerable social limitations. I am also tall, six foot one and a half, to be precise, and I have a big head of curly dark hair, and my glasses are so old that they probably had begun to come back into fashion. On several occasions she sat down at the table with me while I was having coffee in the basement of the chemistry building, where they had a small cafeteria situated.

She never tried to look me in the eyes, and she asked questions, and I would talk at length about my work. There was no give and take, because I cannot operate that way. I fundamentally do not understand the idea of reciprocity. In theory, of course, I do. But in practice I don't know when to talk or not talk, and when someone is getting bored with my monologues.

But we had grown, if not friendly, then familiar to each other over the years. She was, I suspect, interested in me as a specimen of mental disorder. As someone who was clearly outside the realm of "normal," and yet who functioned within the limited scope of academia quite nicely, thank you. I taught my few classes, spent most of my time in the lab with Dr. Liu or in the sciences library, and even, on rare occasions, went out with a few colleagues for a glass of beer.

I did my work efficiently and well.

Very early that spring, some of us were finishing and defending our dissertations, and a number of us had already secured postdoctoral research positions, and a few of us had found tenure-track positions. I found a research position at Case Western Reserve University in Cleveland, which involved very little teaching, which suited me fine. Daniel Schrieber, another of Dr. Liu's acolytes, was hired by the California Institute of Technology, in a tenure-track position, and Susan Grady was hired, tenure-track, at Cornell University, in Ithaca, New York.

All, if I may say, plum positions. Positions of prominence at eminent institutions, with the promise, of course, of advancement, which they have since all taken advantage of.

In the last week of March, those of us who were finishing up, who had found positions, were in an unusually gay mood. Chicago's winters are long and cold, but that week was unseasonably warm. There were a few flowers and buds on the trees, and the sun shined and felt so welcome when you closed your eyes and put your face to it.

Light. Warmth.

I had been several times to dinner with Susan, Daniel,

and Enid Dowd, a chemist who had also just finished and was going to work at Bell Laboratories. We ate our dinners, and it seemed Daniel and Enid were some sort of couple.

On a weekday night, after dinner, we went to a barroom for drinks, something I very rarely did. The bar was just off campus, a quarter mile perhaps from the science quads. I drank two or three beers and I was quite happy, and a little off my guard, if you will.

When we got outside, the night was beautiful and fragrant with flowers and exhaust, garbage, and the very smell of the earth itself. Enid and Daniel took their leave of us, and then Susan did something strange, something I've thought often of over the ensuing years.

She took my arm, when she had not so much as touched me in all the time I'd known her. As we walked toward the quad, she held my arm, and not only was it not unpleasant, I enjoyed the warmth, the gentle pressure, the presence of this tall and rather glamorous woman.

She said she wanted to show me something in her office. She said she'd found some amazing things in PET scans that showed patterns in the brain of violent criminals who were shown very scary photographs.

We walked across the empty quad, and I recall the echo of our footsteps, and thinking how they would echo, those sound waves, for a very long time.

She had the keys to the locked building, and we went to

her third-floor office. Inside it was dark, but she only turned the computer on. She touched my back and neck, and I felt nothing but pleasure. No anxiety, no sense of panic, nothing the least bit awkward. I was outside myself. I was not who I was.

She sat on the edge of her desk, and she said, Trevor.

She took my hands, and drew me to her. She put one hand on the side of my face, and stroked the hair off my cheek.

I've wanted you for a while, she whispered.

She put my hands on her breasts, and I was shocked by how soft they were, and then she leaned forward and kissed me lightly. On the forehead, the neck, then on my lips. Then she kissed me more urgently. I found myself kissing her just as urgently.

She lifted her skirt, and pushed her underwear down. She unbuckled my belt, unbuttoned and unzipped my trousers, and when she spread her legs—I was not myself. It was utter heaven itself. Like nothing I had dreamed could be in this world.

Then it was over.

Susan kissed me. She said, Lovely man.

That is how Levon Grady was conceived.

I was twenty-six years old, we were both twenty-six that spring, and I was not only not a virgin anymore, I was, at least in the biological sense, a father. Of course, I didn't know that at the time.

I never saw Susan Grady again. But I received a card in my mailbox in the physics department some time later. It was a photo of the stars, and inside, Susan wrote, Dearest Trevor—Good luck and congratulations and thank you and goodbye, all at once. I leave for Ithaca tomorrow. I wish all good things for you, and treasure our talks, and finally and at long last, our coming together.

Love, Susan.

I puzzled over the word *love* for a long time. Was that merely a convention, a way of saying, I'm fond of you, a form for *sincerely*, or *best wishes*? Because I was not conversant in the ways, the intricate byways, of love, or of any emotions, for that matter.

As I thought about it, it seemed to me that light was something like human love. How could it be so smooth, so lovely and flowing and warm, the apex of human existence at times, and at other times so gritty, the cause of heartbreak and misery and misunderstanding and even murder?

Did Susan Grady love me? In some way? Some particular convection of pity and affection and attraction and like-mindedness?

Had she planned this final-semester tryst, this conjoining of parts?

What was in her mind?

At any rate, I moved to Cleveland and took up my work, and I received an email from Susan Grady. She wrote that she had thought long and diligently over this, but in the end, after much rumination, she wanted to tell me: that she was pregnant, and that there was no doubt but that I was the father. She expected nothing from me. She had initiated this whole incident. I was in no way responsible.

She had decided to go ahead with the pregnancy, with having the child, and she had plenty of means to raise it on her own. She thought, she said, that I should know. If the positions were reversed, she said that she would want to know.

I thought for several days, and then I wrote back that I didn't know if congratulations were in order, but that I should like to contribute to the child's upbringing, monetarily.

She said that was more than kind, but that it was not necessary. She did not regret the night in question, but she did feel a twinge of guilt about how she had breached my castle, and taken me, as it were, by storm.

We exchanged emails, and after several weeks, we came to an agreement. I would set up a fund, a college fund called a 529, in the child's name and under Susan's control, that sheltered the money from taxes, and to which I would contribute several thousand dollars each year in well-managed growth funds.

I would increase the contributions as my salary grew, and there is now $146,382.17 for Levon Grady to go to college, should he wish to do so.

As a strange footnote, I myself, Trevor Towns, met and married a not-so-young woman, very unlike Susan Grady, who worked in the physics library, more than five years ago. Marie and I are the proud parents of a four-year-old girl named Susan.

Marie knows about Susan and Levon, and she was curiously unconcerned about my tryst, my assignation, years earlier, and she chose the name Susan, which suggests that Marie believed Susan had done something important for me.

We lead a quiet life. Marie cooks, I clean up, and after Susan has been put to bed for the night, I listen to music, using headphones, in the dark living room. I favor the baroque: Scarlatti, Telemann, Handel, but it is Bach who takes me to heaven. The simple sounds of a cello, a piano, a single note, a run of notes, then the repetitions, the intricacies and variations, always so carefully controlled. The way he weaves and reweaves, in unexpected ways, and the patterns occurring, recurring. Hiding, surprising, finding full flower, and it is a night in spring, and the flowers and trees are in bloom, and there is the smell of the earth.

She took my arm, and I seemed to have stepped out of myself. Perhaps, that night, the rest of my life was born. It was like whole other rooms of life existed, of which I had been unaware. It was like for the first time in my life I actually stopped, looked at, and truly smelled a flower.

Twenty-two

Sam

Like blinking eyes and beating hearts, the hours and days and weeks went steadily by. We were in November, and I was feeling pretty darn good, and for me, that was way above average.

Levon was not so hot, at least I didn't think so. He seemed more withdrawn, more inward, and things were roiling inside, and it was hard to tell how or why or exactly what was going on.

Though that wasn't exactly true.

One thing he starting writing about, and it was pouring out, was his father. He started writing how he didn't know his father, had never known his father. Had never seen him, never even seen a picture of him. He didn't know his name, didn't know if he was a serial rapist or killer in prison somewhere in the Midwest, for all he knew. Or was dead. Or sold insurance in California, or surfed in Australia.

From as early as he could remember, his mother had told him that he had no need to know about his father, that it would be bad for him, for Levon, and that his father would never be part of his life. She said to just block that thought, that concept—of a father—out completely, and he'd be happier and healthier.

Occasionally, over the years, he'd ask about or mention his father, and his mother would repeat her mantra. Don't ask. Don't go there. Once, when he was ten or eleven, he pressed her, and he said her eyes got cold, that they had a look almost of meanness behind them. As though she could get very ugly about this, and he was not going to learn anything.

And for the most part, he did block it out, didn't think about it—at least in any conscious, deliberate way. But he'd find himself having dreams about a person he thought was his father. Sometimes he was scary and scarred and had long greasy hair and was about to do something terrible to Levon, and sometimes he was large and kindly, and they were in sunlit fields, or camping in pine woods, and cooking around a small campfire, or watching a baseball game, which was strange because he had never watched a baseball game for more than five minutes in his life.

The thing with Susan was that she was a scientist down to her toes, to the bones in her toes. She believed in facts. She hated ambiguities, and she was certain Levon needed to erase his father from his life, from their life. Case closed.

But the older he got, the more it bothered him. The not knowing. And writing this project made it even worse. Why was she so adamant? So sure? Was she ashamed of something? Afraid of something? Did she really think he would be hurt terribly by knowing who his father was, much less meeting him?

Who knows, he might have the male equivalent of a Vera for a father.

He'd turn eighteen on December 23. He'd legally be an adult. Could he file for a copy of his birth certificate? Was that part of the Freedom of Information Act?

On the other hand, I was writing about having to take riding lessons as a kid, and how the horses terrified me, and how every summer, we rented a house on Martha's Vineyard for a week, and how it was the best times we had as a family together. Dad spent a little time on his Blackberry in the mornings, but the rule was that was it. Only two hours in the mornings. We rode bikes, and Mom tried to teach us to sail, and she really knew what she was doing. She'd been sailing all her life, and it was great to see her in control, confident.

She'd order us to pull on ropes, and duck as the boom swung over our heads, and it was really beautiful and peaceful out there. The sun, the water, the wind, the air, the salty smell, the land and houses growing smaller and smaller, and Dad said, Aren't we getting a little far out here, and Mom smiled and said, Don't worry, honey. I got you covered.

I'd hardly ever seen them that close, and at night we ate lobster and scallops and clams. They even let me drink a little watered-down wine, and the sunsets were something to die for. The sun went down slowly, in these beautiful colors, from orange to purple and lavender and red, and there was like this path of colored light leading to the sinking sun. You felt almost as though you could walk on water all the way to the sun.

At night, in my small bedroom, in the small house, I'd think, Why can't we live here forever? Why can't we stay and be like this? Ride bikes. Walk to places. No shopping, no house designed by the student of some famous architect. Just read books, and not rush around and have Dad work seventy-hour weeks.

And always, on the ferry leaving the island, I felt I was returning to loneliness and sadness and this terrible smothering emptiness.

At home in Ithaca, something really surprising happened at Thanksgiving. In the past we'd always gone out to really fancy restaurants or to my grandparents', with the sherry and old silver. And the shop talk, as Grandpa called it.

Mom and Dad invited a young faculty couple from the business school for Thanksgiving dinner at our house. This was their first year in Ithaca as well, and they had two daughters, who were three and five.

At first I thought, Oh, shit.

Then I thought, Well, this is different.

Mom ordered the turkey cooked and stuffed from Wegmans, the greatest grocery store in the United States, and we made pumpkin pies, and had three vegetables and cranberry sauce and mashed potatoes, and before they arrived, Mom found a box of my old toys in the basement—some dolls and stuffed animals and Legos—and brought them upstairs for the girls.

Dad had a fire going in the fireplace, and then they arrived. Bob and Abby, who looked to be in their midthirties, wore glasses; his were wire-rimmed, hers were retro plastic. They were medium height, and he was a little chunky, had sharp features, and she was slight, blond, pretty, and alert, but looked tired. Her hair was tied back in a ponytail. He had a slightly rumpled sweater on, and she had a blue cardigan over a green dress with a green cloth belt, and I liked them on sight.

And the girls, Ella and Nina. They were gorgeous. Small, with simple dresses and cardigans like their mom, and tights, one red, one green, and Mary Janes. They kind of clung to the mom and dad at first, and my dad said, You like jazz singers, to Bob and Abby, and they laughed, and Abby said, Yeah, and short names that end with A.

We don't know why, but we do, Bob said.

They had brought wine and warm baked bread, which Abby said was kneadless, meaning, you didn't have to knead it.

Then Mom squatted down and said, What pretty dresses, and such pretty names, and one of them said very quietly, You're beautiful, and the other said, And she, pointing to me, looks like a princess.

That's very sweet of you, Mom said, but I don't think we're half as pretty as you two.

I was a little shocked at how gracious and kind Mom could be.

What a start, I thought. I don't think my mom had been so relaxed or gracious in a long time.

Bob went with my dad to open the wine, and Mom said, Would you girls like something to drink?

Sure, they said, and they each took one of Mom's hands and went to the kitchen.

I'm Sam, I said. Formerly known as Samantha.

Abby, formerly known as Abigail.

Come in, I said, Unload, because she was carrying a tote bag.

What a house, she said, and I said, Yeah. It's pretty sweet. Used to be owned by a horticultural professor. The garden's incredible. You gotta see it in the summer.

So how's Ithaca for you? she said.

Curious, I said. We arrived at the same time.

Right.

I've gotta say, I think I like this place a lot. Maybe a real lot. How about you?

The same? Great kid town, down-to-earth, funky, beautiful. But I keep hearing people say you've got to get through your first winter.

They had both come from the University of North Carolina at Chapel Hill, and they liked it there a lot, except for the summers, which were brutally humid. They'd been there six years, after grad school at Cal Berkeley. Bob was at the Johnson School, the B-School, she was a historian, twentieth-century American labor movement, and was in ILR, the School of Industrial and Labor Relations. This was it, she thought. They were here for the duration.

Everyone came back, with wine, and sippy cups for the girls, and Mom handed me a glass of wine that was not watered down. The grown-ups sat around the fire, and I asked the girls if they wanted to see what my mom had found in the basement from when I was their age.

Yes, they said at the same time.

We went over to the couch and chairs by the bay

window, and there were the dolls and stuffed animals and Legos. We got down on the floor, and Nina said she liked the giraffe best, or maybe the rhino, and Ella said the Raggedy Ann doll was cute, and she picked it up, and started to make it talk to a Barbie doll.

You may be pretty, but I've got more hair than you'll ever have, Raggedy said to Barbie.

Barbie said, But I'm skinny and perfect.

You're stiff and perfect, Raggedy said, and you can't cuddle in bed at night.

I laughed, and then we were all three into it. Building Lego footstools for a tiger, a Lego hat for the rhino. Then Ella made a kind of seat of Legos. She bent Barbie's legs, sat her down and said, Look, Barbie has to pee.

We were giggling, and I thought, All three of us hate Barbie. What about that? It was like this unspoken, instinctive bond between us.

We ate dinner, and I felt warm—from wine, from the fire, from playing with little girls, from being with my family, from eating great food. Abby joked in this dark-humored way about how exhausting kids were. It's all food and fluids and sleep deprivation the first two years, she said. It's pure survival.

Mom, Nina said. You love us.

I know, sweetie. I'd give my life for you.

You already have, Bob said, and we laughed.

After dinner we sat on couches and big chairs in front of the fire and sipped wine. Ella wanted to sit in my lap, and I sipped wine very slowly, and soon she was asleep. She was heavy and warm, and I could feel her breath on my neck, and I thought, This whole night has been amazing.

These normal people. These terrific kids. All of us just being people. Then I started thinking, Why can't it be like this all the time? Why does there have to be such awful shit in the world? In my life? In so many lives?

Then I thought, Stop. Stay here.

This moment, the snap and warmth of the fire. The warmth and weight of this lovely kid. Like the ferry back from the Vineyard. A sad, sweet moment. But I wasn't going there.

Right here, I thought again.

Then I wondered what Levon was doing at that moment. I hoped he was doing okay.

Twenty-three

Sierra

Let's face it: Being a teenager sucks. And being in high school, which is a prerequisite for being a teenager, sucks even more. Even if you go to a relatively decent place like the Clock School. Which at least tried to treat you as a more or less normal human being. Which was ironic, of course, because we were the most fucked-up teenagers among all the acne-plagued, angst-ridden, awkward, and goofy teenagers in Ithaca, and the entire United States for that matter.

Okay. I exaggerate. But still.

When you're a teenager, you're not a kid, you're not a grown-up, your hormones are raging, you're sure you'll never fit in anywhere in the world, or you have delusions of happiness and grandeur, which is even more pitiful, because life is gonna fuck you in the ass over and over, and you kind of know it, but you don't either. So no wonder. Who could blame us?

High school might be a tiny bit better than middle school, but not by much.

So I did all this redundant adolescent bullshit such as got tattoos and pierced my ears, nose, belly button, and nipples, but I stopped short of labia. That, even drunk, was too personal. I colored my hair different by the month—red, purple, white-blond, blue—shaved half my head, wore as much leather as possible and boots with four-inch heels, and sneered a good deal.

I smoked filterless Camels and Lucky Strikes, and fucked many boys, and slept with some girls to see what it was like, and listened to baroque music because rock 'n' roll was for kids.

I admit. I was mostly full of shit. But what was an Ithaca kid from a moderately well-off family to do? Dad was an anesthesiologist, Mom taught gender studies at Ithaca College, and they barely blinked. They brought me to doctors, and I swear, it's kind of bleakly funny, in a way—but I was diagnosed at various times as OCD, ADD, narcissistic personality disorder, depressed, bipolar II, and several others I can't recall. The one they missed is the one they hand out at college graduations: B.A. Bad attitude. Or S.B. Spoiled brat. Or just plain B. Bored.

I mean, I had friends, I liked to do things, I played the cello for six or seven years, and that got me going on the baroque. I loved to run and hike, and I love our dog, Hagrid, and I'm embarrassed to admit it, but like every other kid, I loved Harry Potter, and read all of them three times.

Then I started to realize that the characters were pretty broadly drawn. Like Dudley, the fat cousin, and Mr. and Mrs. Dursley, who were so unrelentingly odious, and the Weasleys, who were always such lovely people, poor but honest, and Crabbe and Goyle and Malfoy, who were so predictably noxious and bullying.

I started to think, Plllleeeaaassse. Get me out of here.

I tried Jack Kerouac, who you were supposed to love, and thought, WTF? Then I read what Truman Capote said of him, that this wasn't writing; this was typing. I laughed like hell, and read *In Cold Blood*, which I loved.

I discovered James M. Cain, the great master of American noir. I read *The Postman Always Rings Twice*, and thought, Mother of God. This is hot. Then *Double Indemnity*. I taped a quote from Phyllis over my desk at home:

> *"Maybe I'm crazy. But there's something in me that loves Death. I think of myself as Death, sometimes. In a scarlet shroud, floating through the night. I'm so beautiful, then. And sad. And hungry to make the whole world happy, by taking them out where I am, into the night, away from all trouble, all unhappiness."*

I thought when I first read that, Yeah. Oh, God, I know that feeling.

So, this was supposed to be about Levon, and I could tell you a lot about Levon. I've known him forever. I think we were in the same kindergarten class at Fall Creek, and I've kind of known him since birth. Sometimes he's driven me crazy, because I've been crushing on him almost forever, or half of forever, and sometimes he's made me so fucking mad because he's so withdrawn, and so isolated. Then you'd see him at moments, say with Avery, or Anna, or earlier in the fall with Sam, and he'd seem so normal and charming, and just really, really fucking attractive.

Then you'd go just a little bit near, and the merest touch, the smallest word, and he'd draw inside himself like one of those flowers. The flytrap. Only he'd trap you outside.

I've known Susan a long time too, mostly from a distance, but I tell you, she's the crazy one. She seems so normal, so smart, so beautiful. But I've heard shit over the years, seen shit, and there was very weird stuff going on there.

Like leaving him home alone entire weekends, when he was six or something. Never really letting him have kids over to his house to play. And his father. He knows nothing about his father. His father might be Charlie Manson, for God's sake. Or one of these psychos Susan studies in maxi-max prisons.

And when Levon just cleaned that big asshole's clock at

lunch at the beginning of sixth grade—and I was there; I saw it; it was fucking amazing—and Levon left school for the year. Kids said, Yeah, see. He's got some psycho, serious badass blood. His mom's trying to protect him from killing someone.

After he left sixth grade, and I think it was September, October, he was supposedly homeschooled for the year. I heard his mother let the pediatrician put him on some antidepressant, or some kind of drug, and he saw one psychiatrist one time so he could get certified to come to the Clock School. He got some more meds. But otherwise she wouldn't let the shrinks or psychologists near him.

Because she knows better. She's a brain expert.

And that's the incredible thing I see over and over in this town with professors and doctors. That really, really smart people can often be incredibly stupid.

The thing is, they are smart, often really smart. But it's like some doctors. They don't listen. They ask you a few questions, and then they think they know, because they're trained to read symptoms. But they often don't know, because they're in a hurry, and they're not in your skin. Or so many professors, who may be the world's leading experts on bees or ancient Greek architecture, or they've won the Nobel Prize in physics or economics—their kid's a crack addict and they don't know, or they buy a rear-wheel-drive Benz in Ithaca, which is all but useless in the snow and ice, or they dump their good and sensible wife or husband of twenty-five years to marry an obvious gold-digging bimbo who's into reading tea leaves, and they're sure they're just so smart.

I've seen this over and over. It's like a sitcom, only it's kind of sad too. 'Cause it fucks their kids up as well. I mean, not all doctors and faculty are like this. I overstate to make my point, but you'd sort of assume very smart people would be sensible, but that's very far from the truth.

Plus you throw in the arrogance, and you have some seriously fucked-up individuals, who have done major damage to their kids.

And mark my words. Though she looks good, talks a good game, and is well-known in her field, Susan Grady has done a major number on Levon. I don't know why. But I know a little of the how—isolation and superiority. We are better than everyone else, therefore we must be separate. We are separate, therefore we are superior.

But the truth is, if you're gifted, unusual, superior in that way, you need even more than regular people not to be isolated. You need to be grounded, need to be around other people, need to stay in touch.

Which brings me to Sam, who I have to admit I hated purely on instinct at first. Super-rich, prissy, gorgeous, standoffish. Then I heard she was paired with my boy Levon on this mysterious project, and I loathed her.

But I gotta say, she grew on me. I heard about the hospitals, I saw how hurt she'd been, how very badly damaged. And she had this innate grace and kindness. I may look like a thug, but I sense these things. And I heard, I don't know where exactly, that she had a rich bitch mother who she loathed and who sounded as crazy in some ways as Susan. Do-nothing, shop-in-the-big-city, Benz-driving witch from very old Boston money.

Then I started hoping, maybe she'd reach him. Someone had to. Meg had a chance. Maybe the two of them, Meg and Sam. Who knows.

Me, I'm taking the gap year. Maybe move to the city, maybe move to the country, work on an organic farm. Though I guess you can't smoke cigs there. Which sucks.

But let's face it. Three quarters of me is full of shit. Is an act. Is smoke and mirrors. But at least I know it. And I still love Phyllis, floating in her scarlet shroud at night.

Time, as they always fucking say, as it's ticking away like a bomb, will tell.

Twenty-four

~~~~~~~

Levon

I was gonna turn eighteen December 23, two days before Christmas, not that we ever did much for Christmas. I had always begged Susan for a Christmas tree, and a few times, when I was very young, we got a small fir tree in a small black tub at Wegmans and put a motley string of lights around it. And we did do presents.

She made a big deal of my birthday—made the cake, did the candles, and had lots of presents. But no parties, and I don't think I ever went to other kids' parties, though I was usually invited.

Most years, from age six or seven, we flew to Kansas on the twenty-second or twenty-third, and did the holidays with the Gradys. They lived in a big house in some fairly fancy suburb somewhere northwest of Kansas City. My grandfather is tall and kind of cheerful in this dry way, which always surprised me for a guy who spent his days with corpses and blood-splatter patterns, and possible time of death according to body heat and stomach content. My grandmother is medium height, and must once have been quite striking, and seemed quietly normal, if there ever is such a thing. She still wore dresses around the house, and pearls, even when cooking, and she was funny, in this wry way.

My uncles are both doctors, older than Susan, and had kids of their own, my cousins—two were either surgeons or training to be surgeons, and there was one cousin nobody talked about who had been in and out of rehabs for heroin and crack addiction. Her name was Wendy, and she was tall and quiet and really blond and really gracious the few times I saw her, and always wore long sleeves and long pants, even when we were there in the summer.

In mid-December I got into Cornell ED, early decision, and so did Sam and a few other people we knew. Mom was pretty happy about that, and I was too, because I had no great desire to leave town or go to Brown. I kind of guessed I'd live on campus, at first, in a single, if I could get one.

Then I started worrying about money. How would we pay for this? We got half off tuition because Susan was an employee, but when the financial aid letter came, it said the family was still responsible for over $45,000 a year.

Susan was never a big saver, and I thought, Are we gonna have to take out a huge loan?

You don't have to worry about that, she said.

We were sitting in the front room.

Is grandpa gonna lend us money? Are we gonna win the lottery?

Susan was avoiding my eyes. She looked like she was squirming, something I'd never seen.

What? I said. For fuck's sake, tell me.

I never swore, and she looked like she'd been slapped.

Okay, you prick, she said, and I felt slapped. Because your father has been saving since before you were born, and he has about a hundred and fifty thousand dollars for you.

My father?

She was white-faced.

My father? I said again.

She nodded.

Darth Vader? I asked. Or he who must not be named? Or Charlie fucking Manson? Where the fuck was this coming from? After eighteen years of not a word about this mystery man, he miraculously shows up like the Lone fucking Ranger. I was white with rage.

Don't be silly, she said.

Don't be silly. Don't be fucking silly, I said. Who's been silly for eighteen years? Who created this huge fucking mystery? "You can't know." "It'll never do you any good." And this man, this monster you created in my mind, has been quietly saving, month by month, so his son could go to college. What the fuck?

Don't be dramatic, Levon. And stop saying *fuck*.

But she was actually shaking. She was trembling all over, and she began to tear up, something I know I had never seen.

Why'd you do this, Susan? What's the big mystery? Why'd you have to create this huge fucking void in my mind and fill it with an ogre? What was the point?

She stayed quiet.

I don't even know his name.

You didn't need to know his name. There was no need.

Maybe for you. What about me? Maybe I needed to know his name.

I'll tell you his name on your birthday, in Kansas.

I'm not going to Kansas.

You're what?

Not going to Kansas.

You can't stay here alone.

Are you joking? Are you shitting me? 'Cause I've never been in the house alone? I've been doing that since I was six.

What will you do?

What do I ever do?

She looked over at me, and she was not wet-eyed anymore, and the color had returned to her face.

Your grandparents will be disappointed.

Tell them I have a school project I have to work on.

You sure you want to do this?

What?

Stay home.

Yes. It'll be good for me.

I looked straight at her.

And I want to know my father's name.

She looked away from me. She looked across the room at a Jackson Pollock print. She looked at the ceiling. She looked at the floor, and then she looked back at me.

His name is Trevor Towns. He's a physics professor at Case Western Reserve University in Cleveland. He's very well known in his field. We were graduate students at Chicago together. We had one very brief tryst, shortly before we graduated.

I sat, stunned. I didn't move or say anything for a long time. After a minute, or five minutes, Susan stood up, came over to me, kissed me on the cheek, said, I love you, and left the room.

I sat for a long time.

I thought for a long time. Of Trevor Towns, this physicist. I thought about how from before the time I was born, he had been putting money away so that I could go to college. And he didn't know me any more than I knew him, as far as I knew. Maybe he didn't know my name, and had never even seen a picture of me. Maybe Susan treated him in this matter the way she treated me.

I spent the next few days on the computer, googling Trevor Towns. There were hundreds of hits. He was the Ruth T. Olin chair of physics at Case Western, and his specialty, as far as I could tell, was light. There were dozens and dozens of references to him, to papers he had written, awards he had won. There were even some of his papers online, about fractals and prisms, and the possibility that there could, in theory, be even more dimensions to light than wave and particle if we had the means to heat or cool light, or somehow speed it up or slow it down, fracture or bend it, use prisms and a long series of complex, powerful mirrors, or subject it to severe gravity.

I didn't really get any of it. There were lots of complex equations and strange diagrams, and he seemed to co-author a number of papers with two professors, one at Caltech and another at Yale.

He was a member of the National Academy of Sciences, had been born in East Anglia, UK, graduated from Manchester University in the UK, then earned his Ph.D. at the University of Chicago in 1996, when he assumed his position as assistant professor at Case Western. He was married and had a daughter.

I clicked on images, and holy shit! There he was. He looked a lot like me. Or rather, I looked a lot like him. Tall, with unruly hair that was curlier and darker than mine, the same nose and mouth and ears, even similar glasses, but his looked a bit darker and heavier, the lenses thicker. There were shots of him at a podium, receiving or giving out a plaque, some award, of him lecturing, of him in front of a whiteboard with crazy huge equations. There were pics of him with students, apparently at receptions, with colleagues, because they all looked like science people, in a coat and tie, in another pic in a short-sleeved shirt, and he had surprisingly powerful forearms, a farmer's forearms.

I kept looking, and reading. I checked if he had a Facebook page, but he didn't, then if there was a Wikipedia article about him, and there was.

I kept closing my computer, and lying on my futon, and thinking, What was Susan thinking? What could she possibly have been meaning to do? Surely she was afraid of something, or ashamed, but Susan was not one for shame or fear.

And now what was I gonna do?

Go to school and say, Hey, guess what? I have a father, and he's an interesting guy. Some kind of big deal in physics.

Meanwhile, the semester was winding down; Ithaca was emptying out, the way it did every winter break, starting around mid-December, and every summer. The students would start to leave, and by the twentieth of December or so, the town became slow and sleepy and silent and lovely.

It became something different entirely. The few winter breaks I'd spent here had been gorgeous, quiet, almost holy. Hours could go by, and not a single car would pass on North Tioga Street, where we lived.

I hadn't spoken to Susan since the night of the big revelation. She'd asked me a few times if I was okay, and I'd nodded. She nodded, got almost teary once or twice.

She left early for the 5:45 flight on my birthday, and said she'd get a cab. She'd hugged me hard the night before. She said, You're eighteen. You can vote now.

She said she'd call, then said good night, and she looked sad.

She had left me a wrapped package and an envelope on the dining room table that I found when I woke up around ten on my birthday. The package was this beautiful black mackintosh coat I'd been wanting, and it was XL Tall. It fit perfectly, was pure wool, and the back and shoulders had been treated to resist rain and snow. The card was an Ansel Adams winter scene. Happy Birthday, Sweetheart, she wrote. With much love; signed, Susan. And there were five crisp one-hundred-dollar bills inside. Beaucoup bucks. A whole new level of cash.

I wandered around the house, from room to room to room. I put some music on, first Radiohead, then the Smiths, then I had this urge for some sacred music. I put Mozart's Requiem on, and turned it up loud.

I'm an atheist, I suppose, but I've always loved sacred music. Bach and Beethoven's Masses, Purcell, even the great early English composer Thomas Tallis, who composed masses and used polyphonic voices that made my spine shiver.

I felt weird, and wondered if I should try some of Susan's booze. But the little drinking I'd tried had always made me dizzy and kind of sick. Then I went to the medicine cabinet in the second-floor bathroom. There were about a half dozen amber pill containers. There was sertraline, which I somehow knew was her antidepressant, and amoxicillin, an antibiotic. But there were three containers that had the controlled substance warning, and I knew that meant they were the interesting ones. They could give you a buzz. One was alprazolam. Take one tablet at bedtime for insomnia. Another was clonazepam. Take one tablet as needed for anxiety. And the third was hydrocodone. Take one tablet as needed for pain.

I decided to try one of each. A little chemical cocktail for my eighteenth birthday. Why not? I thought. I'm eighteen.

So I took one of each, went to the third floor, where my phone and computer were, and waited, lying on the futon. Nothing happened.

I was checking through Facebook, seeing where people were going for break, and it seemed as though quite a few were leaving town. Not only did most of the students get out of town, but many of the faculty and staff families left to visit people in other places.

I wondered if my father stayed in Cleveland, or went to East Anglia. I knew Sam would be around, and Anna was staying, and so were Avery and Sierra. Meg was going away for maybe a weekend, but was mostly gonna be around.

I checked my watch. Fifteen minutes had passed, and I had to say, the drugs had proved to be a disappointment. I thought that maybe I should break with tradition, with my entire life, and actually call some people, or take a walk and get coffee the way Sam and I did once. Invite them over for—

What did people do? Talk? Drink? Smoke cigs? Have sex? I was eighteen, and I'd never even kissed a girl. Not really. Girls had run up to me on a dare and kissed me, but that didn't count. It was all pretty sad. Jejune. That was the word. Unsophisticated. Dull. That had been on the SAT. I'd nailed it.

Then I was starting to feel something. Something relaxed. Something pleasant. Something warm, almost sweet. A little floaty. A bit euphoric. Happy. Really loose and a little tired. But nice. Like the world was nice, and people were nice, and everything was pretty much good all over. Just warm. Just lovely.

So this was drugs. This was what the fuss was all about.

I could hear Mozart, and God, oh, God, it was splendid. The Sanctus. The Benedictus.

I was floating, but getting sleepy too. And I was happy because I had a father. But sad too because for all those years I had not had one. Part of me was high as the sky, but part of me was watching me, and there I was on my eighteenth birthday, and I was on the third floor, buzzed on drugs, and feeling kind of new and good. But also not so good, because I was the way I always was, and that was alone. And even with the pills, or maybe because of the pills, I felt something.

I went downstairs and took another of each of those pills. What the hell. It was the holidays. I think I took two more Christmas morning.

I felt alone. A speck, floating by itself in this great sea of human beings. That's what it looked like from a distance anyway. Just alone and alone and more alone. The way it had always been. But it didn't feel distant anymore. It felt sad. And even though I didn't, the way I never did, it made me want to cry.

Twenty-five

~~~~~

Sam

I wrote my college essay on the year I spent at McLean and Austen Riggs. I figured, What the hell. I couldn't just skip that year; it wasn't on my transcript, and Meg said it was a show of strength, and if someone in an admissions office saw it as a negative, it was more than offset by my SATs. Plus, it was part of what I was, for better or worse. Take me or leave me.

Then I got into Cornell ED. I was pretty happy. I didn't want to leave Ithaca so soon. It was growing on me, even as the winter set in. I had heard a lot about the Ithaca winters. How long and cold and gray they were. How unrelenting. But I wasn't exactly from Miami or Phoenix. I was from Boston. We had winters there.

So the city started to empty out, just like in the summer, only cold. And almost everyone I knew, my friends, were going to be around. Mom and Dad and I were going to stay put too, and that made me happy. If Christmas was half as good as Thanksgiving, then I was content. Abby and Bob were going to see relatives somewhere, but Mom and Dad invited a few foreign grad students for dinner, early Christmas afternoon. One from China, one from the UK, one French, and one Irish.

I knew somehow that Levon had a birthday two days before Christmas, and then I heard that he had refused to go to Kansas with Susan, to see her family, the way they'd done almost every year. He was staying home, celebrating by himself.

Levon celebrating?

It kind of worried me. Some serious shit seemed to be going on with him, and it wasn't just about his father; now he and Susan were not getting along. When I asked him about that, he paused and said, Let's just say I'm realizing how fucked up she is.

Then he walked away.

It was like there were storm clouds surrounding him, and he was even more distant than ever.

Avery and Anna said they always thought something was kind of off about Susan, and they said they weren't the only ones. This whole thing about Levon not having a father. That his father might be dead, or some psycho killer or mysterious figure who could not be known or named. How weird was that?

Sierra, who I had begun to kind of like and respect and even hang out with a little, said there was nothing wrong with Levon that couldn't be laid at the feet of fucking Susan.

We were having our last coffee on the afternoon before break, and Sierra had gotten hold of some Gauloises, these French smokes that could tear your lungs out, but were very cool because they were what everyone smoked in French New Wave movies back in the '50s. We sipped and shivered and talked about getting together over break, and I said that maybe we should try to get Levon to come out, should do something together, all of us.

Sierra and Anna laughed, and said, Good luck with that.

Avery said, Honey, you haven't known him very long. We'd love to, but it just won't happen.

At home we had a tree, which Mom and Dad and I actually cut ourselves on a tree farm. I was freezing my ass off, and Mom said maybe we should have just gone to one of the places on the strip on Route 13, with flags like a used-car place. But Dad was gung-ho, and Mom and I called him Nanook of the North, and we laughed and froze, but it was kind of fun.

Once it was up and decorated, it was lovely, and then Mom ordered the turkey from Wegmans, of course, 'cause Mom couldn't cook a turkey to save her life.

Mom and Dad seemed to be doing pretty well, but I'd

still hear yelling behind closed doors once in a while, and one weekend she spent two days in bed. She claimed she had a cold, but I could tell she was depressed or pissed off, or Dad had done or said something—maybe about her parents, or maybe she just felt really, really down. Depression didn't just disappear, even if it improved. Maybe it was just hard to be grown-up and married.

I called Levon three times on his birthday, left messages, said I had a few presents for him. I'd gotten him a copy of DeLillo's *Mao II*, which he hadn't read, and I knew he'd love, and I burned him copies of Radiohead and the Pogues, which were two of my favorite bands.

But no answer, and no callback.

I called again Christmas Eve. I said, Levon, would you please call me?

But nothing.

Then on Christmas we opened presents, and it was all pretty nice. I hate the word *nice*, but it was. There were sweaters, coats, electronic stuff, some jewelry, but not as much as in past years. Then we did dinner around two, and the grad students who were staying in Ithaca for the holidays came over and they were all a little awkward. But we plied them with wine, and loosened them up, and they told jokes, and Mom said, No talk about business, and Dad said, You each have to tell a funny story about home.

The Irish woman's story was best—about a skinny

chicken that was supposed to be Christmas dinner, and got away, and she and three brothers had to chase it for at least a mile through fields in the country, and finally gave up, figuring it had more than earned its life. They all had to take baths before dinner. We laughed, and ate, and the fire was going.

By the time they were gone, it was dark.

Both Mom and Dad said they were going upstairs for a nap, and I thought, Hmmm.

Then I didn't want to think about it.

It was five, and then six, and I was sipping wine very slowly, and I tried Levon again. Still no answer.

Finally I thought, Fuck it.

Christmas nights are always a little sad anyway. Like the time after a party. Empty cups, and full ashtrays, and everything a mess. Not that our place looked so bad at all. I cleaned up a little, then I thought again, Fuck it.

I left a note, saying I was going to Anna's for a while.

I got my coat and bag, and Levon's presents. Outside was cold and clear, but the car started up, no problem. I knew where he lived, had driven by his house a bunch of times, and I even knew that they kept a spare key under the front doormat. He'd written that somewhere.

I drove down the hill and there were no cars on the road at all.

I parked in front of his house, and it was completely

dark. There were two or three houses with lights on in the entire block.

I got out, walked up the creaking steps to the porch, and rang the bell and waited. Nothing. One minute, two minutes. I rang again, waited again.

Then I thought once more, Fuck it. Maybe it was the wine. Maybe it was fear. Or love. Maybe it was all those things. But I felt around under the mat, found the key on a ring, opened the storm door, and tried the lock.

My hands were shaking. This was actually illegal, wasn't it?

But the key fit; I turned it, opened the door, and went inside.

Everything was silent. I knew he slept on the third floor like me. I paused and listened, just in case Susan had not gone out of town. But all I could hear was the hum of the refrigerator, and the furnace below.

My eyes got used to the dark. I could see polished wood floors. Bookcases, chairs and couches and lamps. The rooms were small, but the house seemed to be deep, like there was room after room. The stairs were immediately on my right. They were carpeted.

I went slowly up, and these stairs didn't creak. There was light from a streetlight falling through a window on the second-floor hall. There were lots of doors. An office, a small bedroom, a bathroom, another doorway on the left, then another, and that was a big bedroom, with another big room beyond that room. I backed up, went to the second doorway on the left, opened the door, and there was a steep flight of carpeted stairs. At the top I could see bookshelves, and a skylight.

I started up the stairs, and I could feel his presence. I could hear his slow breath, and my heart was beating like a hummingbird.

What am I doing? I thought. Then I thought, I don't give a shit.

At the top was a long room with slanted ceilings, two skylights, a railing around the stairs, three big windows behind a desk that looked onto the street, and bookshelves that ran the entire length of the room on both sides, just below where the ceiling slanted. And in a corner was a big futon on the floor, and sleeping deeply, under a mountain of blankets, was Levon Grady, Birthday Boy, Mr. Yuletide, Man of Mystery.

I took my coat and boots off, got the wrapped book and burners out of my bag and set them on a chair. Then I walked carefully to the futon and sat on the edge. There were Buddhist prayer flags hanging over the three front windows, and prints and cards on the wall, most of which I could hardly make out. One was a Vermeer, the pregnant woman reading a letter, another one was that eerie *Empire of Light* by Magritte, which I'd once seen at the Museum of Modern Art.

It was beautiful and peaceful and strange.

There were clothes in neat piles, and books and books and more books, and Levon's phone and computer were on top of the bookcase near the futon.

Hey, I whispered.

Levon, I said, a little louder.

But his breathing was deep and even, and he didn't stir.

I put my hand on his shoulder, on top of the blankets, and shook him a little.

Hey, pal, I said.

Then I slid my hand under the blanket, and he was warm as a bear. I rubbed his shoulder, then I began to move my hands in his hair, that wild unruly mess of hair.

Levon, I said. Wake up. It's Christmas.

Mmmm, he said.

It's Christmas and your birthday, and you're sleeping your life away. C'mon.

Whaaaaaa, he said.

Levon, it's Sam. I'm here on a mission.

Sam? he said, still half asleep.

Your friend and co-conspirator. The girl who's been calling you.

Oh, damn.

Damn what?

I'm sorry.

Don't be sorry.

How'd you get in here? How'd you know—?

I knew Susan was away, and you wrote somewhere that she left a key under the front doormat. And I knew you weren't going to Kansas, so you'd be here hanging with all your friends.

You've been drinking, he said, and laughed.

We had wine with dinner. And I sipped a little while I cleaned up a bit. Just a buzz.

God, I tried a few of Susan's pills. Slept a lot. I still feel kind of buzzed. Loosey-goosey.

He sat up, his back against the wall.

Mind if I get under the covers? I said. It's a little chilly up here.

What the hell, he said, and lifted the covers.

I got under the covers, my back to the wall, to the pillows. He must have had a half dozen pillows.

So this is where it all happens? I said.

He smiled.

This is where it happens, he said. Or fails to happen.

The inner sanctum, the lair, the aerie.

I like those. Maybe aerie's the best.

I brought you some presents. Just some minor birthday and Christmas stuff.

I handed him the two packages wrapped in silver paper.

Should I open them?

I nodded.

He opened *Mao II*, and read the first page.

Jesus, he said. Why didn't I know about this?

'Cause you didn't know me.

Then he opened the burners. I love them, he said. Should I put one on?

Sure. Put on *In Rainbows*, but skip the first two tracks. They're kind of loud when you're waking up.

He got up, and he was wearing cut-off sweatpants and a T-shirt. I couldn't help noticing how long and beautiful he was.

Then "Nude" came on, and Thom Yorke's weirdly beautiful voice. Gliding, whispering, soaring, silent.

Boy, he said, back under the covers.

You like?

I think.

You mind if I hold your hand? I said.

Really?

I've been wanting to do that for a while.

Please do, he said.

I'm not trying to put any moves on you. I don't know any moves.

Nor do I.

I just couldn't stand the thought—

Of?

You here alone.

I've done a ton of it.

I gathered, I said, and laughed. I've done some too.

It gets—

Boring?

Alone?

Repetitious?

Redundant?

Un-fun?

Could I make a request? he said. Purely as friends.

Of course.

Can I put my arm around you?

That might be nice.

So he did, and Thom Yorke sang, and I said, This is a sweet room, and my fingers played with his hair.

Then I was getting really warm. I said, I've gotta take my scarf and sweater off, and I did, and I said, I'm not trying to seduce you. I promise. I'm a virgin too.

Why are you so sure—?

We listened to Radiohead, and I said, But maybe, to kind of make up for your birthday and Christmas, I could spend the night. Just you and me. Familial, not erotic.

Hunh?

You know? Plato or Aristotle's three kinds of love: spiritual, familial, and erotic.

What about your parents?

I'll call, tell them I'm at Anna's.

You sure?

Very sure.

Then yes. Very yes.

Lemme get my phone.

You need a light?

No. This should all be done under cover of darkness.

I gotta use the bathroom, he said. He got up and went downstairs, and I texted Mom. Am spending night at Anna's. Love, S.

Then just in case, I texted Anna, I'm spending the night at yr place if anyone asks. Talk later.

Then I took off my top and jeans, my socks, and was under the covers in my underthings when Levon came back. He had washed his face and brushed his teeth. He was minty.

He slid under the covers and said, Holy shit, and I said, Familial, remember, but why don't we try kissing? We're both a little buzzed.

His lips were soft and warm, and we were slow and very tentative. Light, and just touching, and then we used our tongues.

This is unbelievable, he whispered, and I kept saying, Sweet Levon, and he said, Lovely, lovely, lovely, over and over again.

Sometime very late, near dawn, I think, we fell asleep. And that was my first Christmas in Ithaca.

Twenty-six

~~~~~~~

Trevor

New Year's Day. I had just received the most extraordi-
nary email. It began, Dear Professor Towns, aka Father,
aka Dad—

He had said that his name was Levon Grady, and that
two weeks ago he found out from his mother, Susan Grady,
that I was his father. He had never known my name, or
who I was, or if I was dead or alive. He hadn't known if I
was a killer in some prison from Susan's early research, or
if I was a salesman at Sears, or if I was an airplane pilot or
a chef or a gas station attendant in Ohio or Miami or some
town near Sioux Falls, South Dakota.

He hadn't known what I looked like, if I lived in a split-
level suburban ranch house, or a trailer park, or under a
bridge, or in an apartment house in Wheeling, West Virginia.
Or Australia or Amsterdam or Vienna, for that matter.

He knew I had once existed, because he existed. But that

was all. He had always wondered. He had asked from a very early age, and Susan had always made it very clear that I was not a part of their lives, that it would not be a good thing if I were, and that I would never be part of their lives.

So forget it, she always said. It didn't matter. Don't even think about it.

So he tried not to.

He tried hard. And for the most part, during the days, he didn't. At least not consciously. But he dreamed about me all the time. He wrote, Sometimes you were a very scary monster, almost like the devil, with fangs, and long greasy hair, and you were always about to hurt me. But sometimes you were a good guy, and we were throwing a baseball back and forth, or walking along a street, or hiking through these sunlit woods, and just sitting and laughing at something stupid. Once I dreamed we were watching a baseball game on television, even though I don't watch or know anything about baseball.

But you never went away, even in the days, he continued. Just about every day there was a moment, a few seconds, sometimes minutes or hours, when I thought about you, and who you were, and where you might be, and if you knew I existed, and if you didn't want anything to do with me.

If that was Susan's choice, or your choice, or the choice of both of you.

That took me aback. To hear he was tormented by the idea that I didn't want him to know about me.

Every once in a great while he'd ask Susan about me. And she'd get steely. Cold, with the threat of meanness, though she'd never been mean. She's just extremely confident, very sure. She's a scientist. She knows facts, she presents evidence. This is proven, and can't be unproven, or even questioned.

But now he knows. He got into college, into Cornell, early decision. And he asked, How can we pay for this, aside from her faculty discount? It would still cost tens, even hundreds of thousands of dollars.

She said, Don't worry. Your dad has been saving for college for you since before you were even born. He wrote, And I thought, I actually said, What the fuck? (Excuse my language.)

She told him the basic facts. My name, the fact that I'm a physicist at Case Western, and that he was conceived from a single act of intercourse just before we left Chicago.

He said he looked up everything he could about me on the Internet. He tried to read articles I'd published. He saw pictures of me, and he said we even looked alike.

Then he didn't know what to do. He wasn't sure if I was like Susan, if I, Trevor, wanted nothing to do with him, as she wanted him, Levon, to have nothing to do with me, Trevor.

But he felt he wanted to at least thank me for saving all

that college money. That had to mean something. To put money away every few weeks for eighteen years. That had to mean that I cared, didn't it? Or felt responsible, at least.

It was all very confusing.

He was relieved I wasn't in a prison. And he felt very proud that I was such a distinguished professor. In physics. He said he was always considered smart in school. That he read books constantly, and was considered kind of weird. That he had very few friends. Or no real friends in some way. That Susan had always been superprotective of him. Kind of crazy-protective.

And here I almost felt like crying. I felt my heart go out to him. It had gone out to him from Dear Professor Towns, aka Father, aka Dad. But now it was a storm, a typhoon of emotion. I wanted to call him. I wanted to book a flight to Ithaca, New York, or tell him to book a flight to Cleveland.

How could I explain Susan to him? Who I only partly knew. Who I had thought about so much over these two decades. How could I tell him that I thought of him, maybe as much as he thought of me? That I was as foolish and wrong as Susan? That I should have insisted on seeing him? That I should have been brave, assertive?

But that there were so many things, so many years. That grown-ups, even though we appear to know and understand things, are as baffled and at sea as children much of the time. That we are lost. That we don't know what we are doing, despite the best intentions. That we, too, were children once, and remain so as adults. At least in many respects. That love, like light, is both wave and particle. All my adult life I have been searching for ever more dimensions of light. I believe it may be more than wave and particle. It may bend, and it may involve heat and time and vast spaces. Immense perspectives may play a part in our perception of it.

So I hit respond.

Dear Levon, aka Son, I began.

Where to begin? I was terribly moved and honored by your good and eloquent and searing email. I am glad to contribute to your Cornell education. It's the least I can do, and it's a fine school. Congratulations!

But where to begin?

I did not know Susan well. We were friends at best. But I had no real friends at Chicago. Like you, I was very isolated. I believe Susan thought I was somewhere in the middle of the Asperger's spectrum, which is a form of autism.

I came from a desperately poor family in East Anglia, in England. That's in the far eastern part of the country. My family were tenant farmers, which is roughly the British equivalent of sharecroppers, even into the early 1980s, hard as that may be to believe. We lived in what was little more than a shack, and we lived more or less at the farmer's whim, on his land, in his shack, working, all of us, my mother and father, my older sisters and brother, very, very hard.

I was the youngest of four, and the youngest by some stretch. The next oldest above me, my sister Mary, was seven years older than me. I was, they said, an afterthought.

This was a very remote farm, nearly ten or twenty kilometers from the nearest town, and we had no electricity and no indoor plumbing until I was seven, when we moved to Harwich, in Essex, so that everyone except me could take jobs in factories. We lived in public housing, which had electricity, running water, and Mother and Father, and James and Elizabeth, the two oldest, all found factory work. Within a few years, my family took a mortgage out on a semidetached house. Whatever we were, my family were very hardworking people.

I have always carried those early years in my head. The idea that we were little more than peasants, that we shivered in winters, took baths in a tin tub once a week, in water heated on a single coal-fired stove, and that coal was very dear. The stove heated the house, was used to cook on, and our clothes were threadbare, patched, and handed down.

In summers we bathed in a nearby creek.

But I was a gifted child in school. Silent, awkward, acutely aware of my peasant status, I was nonetheless always the head of every class, particularly when we arrived in Harwich. I won ribbons and medals in every subject, and my teachers asked Mother and Father to come in for a conference. I don't know what was said, but the result was that I sat for examinations for public schools (the term for private schools in the UK), and for scholarships. I won scholarships to several, and went to a middling preparatory school (or high school) in Norwich, where again, I excelled, and was encouraged to sit exams. I did so well that I could have gone to Oxford or Cambridge, but my headmaster said they were too class-bound, and that I would be fine at the University of Manchester.

Again, the pattern repeated itself. I excelled, took firsts in mathematics, physics, and chemistry, and as graduation approached, the dean of students recommended I go to America for postgraduate study. It was more democratic, less posh. He further recommended that I not go to any of the famous East Coast universities such as Princeton or Yale, but to the University of Chicago. He had a friend there, and he said Chicago was intellectually elite—Fermi and Teller had been there—and had vast sums of money, but that Chicago was America's most democratic city. He quoted the poet Carl Sandburg. "Hog Butcher for the World." "City of the Big Shoulders."

So I won a prestigious fellowship to Chicago that paid for everything for five years—tuition, fees, room and board, even my airplane ticket.

In Chicago, I met your Susan, and fell under the sway of

a famous mathematician and physicist named Frank Liu. Chicago, the city, was everything the dean said it would be, but it was a case of severe culture shock. Five or ten times the size of Manchester, bustling, friendly, and back-slapping, and the university was intensely rigorous. Local wags said it was the university where fun went to die.

Your mother, who was beautiful and conspicuous and glamorous—imagine a tall blond beauty studying the MAO-A gene, the so-called Psychopath or Warrior Gene—and I was strangely, awkwardly known because I was Frank Liu's protégé, studying light, looking for further dimensions of something so omnipresent, so basic, and at the same time so mysterious.

I was friendless, poor, intensely aware of how poor I was, of what odd clothes and glasses I wore, of how I utterly lacked social skills, and above all, I was intensely shy, and suffering, as I said, from the shock of the new.

Susan, for some reason, sought me out. Maybe she found me interesting. A specimen. Possibly attractive. Certainly different. And yes, brilliant.

Perhaps I do have some slight touch of Asperger's. Many good scientists do. But she knew nothing about my background, my poverty, the tin bath, the lack of electricity.

We drank coffee once in a while, and in our last year, with another couple, we had dinner a few times.

Not long before we were to leave Chicago, when we had

all been granted our degrees and had found very good jobs at eminent universities, after a dinner and a few more drinks than usual, she seduced me.

I never saw her again.

In the summer, she sent me an email from Ithaca, told me she was pregnant and intended to keep the child, but that she was absolutely going to do this on her own. I said I respected her decision, would start a college fund for the child, and over the years we have had very little contact.

A few times I asked about you via email. Asked for a photograph, wanted to know for sure what your name was, but she refused all information. She said only that the child was fine, but that it was best that we not know anything about each other.

Why?

I don't know. I thought often about it, and at times I thought of pressing the issue, and at times I have been ashamed that I did not. Perhaps I assumed you did not want any contact, just as Susan did not.

I don't know why Susan seduced me. Because of genuine affection. Because it was exciting and we were a little tipsy, and she wanted to break through my aloneness. Because she wanted genuine contact, she wanted to give me something. Because it was an experiment, to see what two very bright people might produce.

But why this obsession to keep us apart? To have us know

nothing about each other? Susan is a scientist, as I am. She is an expert in the brain. But I wonder sometimes if she realizes that the heart, as a metaphor, is part of the brain. That our feelings, our memories, our spirit, our soul, if you will, reside in the brain. And we must attend to the matters of the metaphorical heart with information and knowledge. The brain and the heart cannot be so clearly separated.

I have gone on too long. Let me close by saying that I very much hope we can talk more. Via email, telephone. Perhaps when you are ready, in person. We have, as they say, a great deal to catch up on. But please do know that you have always, every day, been in my thoughts.

Your loving father,

aka Professor Towns, aka Trevor, aka Dad

Twenty-seven

Anna

Sam told me the whole story, about going to his house Christmas night, slightly drunk, through empty streets. It had to be slightly drunk, and it had to be empty streets, the feeling that nobody was watching, because otherwise there was no way she would have done such a thing.

Even so, she felt like she was half-crazy, she couldn't believe she was doing it even while she was doing it. She half expected Susan to jump out from behind a corner, or sirens and swirling red lights to appear. But nothing happened at all.

And all the time, of course, she had no idea how he'd react. If he'd go nuts, or cold, or kick her out. But he was so sweet, so grateful. And though there was no sex, she slept there. The entire night. In his bed. His futon. With him. With Levon Grady. The untouchable.

But since then, she had had no idea what the fuck was going on, why he was really distant and seemed kind of tormented. Two steps forward, sweet as honey. Then three and a half steps sideways, four backward, one and a quarter forward. She talked to Meg one-on-one about Levon, she talked to Ron, the school psychologist, good old Ron, and they both said, Patience. Said he'd been dealing with some stuff she didn't know about.

So they kept meeting twice a week, and I began to spend nights at Sam's place, or she stayed over at my place, and she started to tell me about the year in the mental hospitals.

How she'd cut herself at Groton, had shock treatment at McLean and the weird, electric, buzzy feeling you had in your brain for days. Fuzz and buzz, and clouds, with bolts of lightning. How her dad had worked at Fidelity and Harvard, and how her mom was kind of nuts. She hated all of it. This giant hole in all their lives.

And Austen Riggs, and how much she actually liked it there. How she no longer had shock treatment, and within a month of getting there in late December, they let her have most privileges. They moved her from the second to the third floor where she could have her own room, and she had tutors, who were usually seniors from Smith or Mount Holyoke, and she read all these amazing books.

The Berkshires, in western Massachusetts, were maybe her favorite place in the world, after Ithaca. And her doctor was an Indian woman, Sylvia Singh, who had been raised in England, and had a wonderful British accent, and was so kind, and had huge brown eyes, and laughed. She was afraid, sometimes, she was falling in love with Dr. Singh.

Aren't you supposed to? I said.

In a way, I guess.

Then she turned on her side, because we had both been lying on Sam's bed, and said, And you, Anna? What about you?

It was late and dark. It was February vacation, and it had been unbelievably cold. It had been below zero at least a dozen nights in the new year, sometimes as low as twenty-two below, and nineteen below, and highs during the day of minus one, or zero, or two above. The windchills were off the charts.

Sam had a queen-size bed, and we were under about four layers of wool blankets and down comforters, and I started playing with her hair.

Why are you always so sane and even and cool? Sam asked.

No, I'm not, I said.

You know Avery says you're the coolest person in the school, but nobody notices because unlike Sierra, or himself, or Levon, you fly below the radar in your cooldom.

Right, I said.

He said you dress better, with more style, and don't even

try. You have the most beautiful skin, you're insanely bright, but never show off, you take calculus, play multiple musical instruments—

Please, I said.

And, moreover, he said you have more genuine kindness, are more trustworthy and compassionate, by far, than anyone in the school. And Avery should know.

But who wants to be a bridesmaid?

You'll be a bride. You have no idea how cool you are. And you're my first and only friend. That sure as hell matters to me.

It does to me too, Sam. A great deal.

We were quiet, and we could feel the cold and dark outside. It must have been two a.m. and five below.

But I want a boy, she said.

I want a boy too, I said.

And you'll probably get him.

Last year, I said, there were moments, a number of times, when I'd be sitting in one of the quiet rooms, and nobody was around. Say it was late, and I'd be reading, or doing something on my computer, and Noah would come in and sit down, and he wouldn't say anything for a while.

I'd look up, smile, but I wouldn't say anything either. And it was so weird. He'd just sit, and watch me, kind of half smiling, or semiserious, and sometimes it would last for a half hour. And there were moments when I wanted to stand up and go over, and just start kissing him, and stroking him, very slowly and gently. I felt that at that moment he would have let me. I felt as though he knew how I felt, he would have lain back in his chair and let me kiss and stroke him. And I fantasized about it, about unbuttoning his shirt and unzipping his pants, and making him moan and beg.

I kept thinking, This boy has never been touched. I wanted to shock and awe him with what pleasure I could give him.

I shouldn't even be telling you these things, but it happened, these times when he came in, and sat down, and watched me, and I just kept on doing what I was doing. And I was never sure what he was doing. If he thought anything along the lines I was thinking. Because I had such a bad crush on him, and I was just a girl with raging hormones, and it had been like that for months, and I'd been so good.

Am I making sense? I asked.

Sam nodded, and then whispered, Very much so.

And in a way, I still regret that I didn't do anything. That I was a nice girl.

You're not a nice girl, she whispered. She reached, and touched my breasts. You've made me very, very hot, she whispered.

Have I? I said softly.

We touched, and kissed lightly, and it grew more and

more intense, then I thought, My God, don't stop, don't stop, and she was soaking, and the wind and cold were far away, and later, much later, she said, Now that was some surprise.

And kissing her neck, holding her, I said, Indeed. Had we been talking about a boy?

Twenty-eight

~~~~~~~~

Avery

It was pushing toward spring, or what passes for spring in Ithaca, and I don't know what it was, but something was going on with Levon. Maybe it had to do with this secret project. Lots of us had been asked to write these kind of top-secret reports for Meg, as part of the thing where Meg and Sam and Levon were working on this yearlong project that absolutely nobody could read—and that drove me crazy, the not knowing—but Levon was changing.

Not completely. Not that he was no longer Levon, or that he didn't look more or less the same, but I swear, he was definitely different, and in kind of large and small ways.

Now remember, I'd known him pretty much forever, since he was a little kid, and while there were tons of weird kids in school, in a way every kid was kind of weird in one way or another—take me, for example, or Sierra or even

Anna, who seemed pretty normal, but was really pretty quirky in her way—we were all a bunch of weirdos.

We had twitches and tics, we were goofy and awkward, we tried so, so hard to fit in and find our way through the hell that is childhood, and especially teenager-hood, that we just fucked it up. Wore the wrong clothes, or too much makeup, or not enough makeup, or we were acne-plagued and full of angst, and it came out in all of us. We said stupid things, or were really mean to other kids, in ways that you just would not be as a grown-up.

I'd bet that at least a quarter, maybe a third, of the kids in the Ithaca City School District were on some kind of psychiatric med—Adderall or Ritalin, Prozac or Effexor or something—so how could you say anybody, any kid, was normal?

But Levon had always been in a category all his own. So physically beautiful, so brilliant, but so withdrawn, so alone and friendless, and that mother, Susan, Ms. Expert in psycho killers, and the secret of his father, which must have really eaten away at him. And never going out. Just being alone in that house, and never going to parties.

But gradually, almost without anyone noticing, Levon was becoming different, as though they'd found a new med for him, though I was pretty sure this had nothing to do with meds. Susan would not have allowed that.

Levon was walking around as though he had oil in his

joints. Before he moved kind of stiffly, as though everything was rusty and tense, but now he was looser, more flowing. And you'd hear his laugh, and you'd see him in the halls, stopping to talk to people, and you'd actually see him smile a lot. And that was something I noticed last.

Levon's smile. He had beautiful, perfect white teeth, and I realized I'd hardly seen them in all the years, because he so rarely opened his mouth, and he almost never smiled. And he had this wonderful, infectious smile. Where not only did his beautiful teeth show, but you'd see the smile in his eyes, in his whole face. And he was so damned handsome.

It was also the way he'd sit down with people at lunch. The way he made little jokes and comments, which were always really smart and sly. And I think other people noticed too.

It was like our crown prince was emerging from his cocoon.

I speculated, of course, because that's what I do. That's my nature and it's my job, in a way. And I had to think of two things, two things that were related.

Sam Vash, and this big secret project with Meg and Sam. They were doing something that was getting to him. Doing something that was getting very deeply at his soul, if there is such a thing. Because Meg was the kind of teacher who could do that. And she was putting a lot of time into this project, and she was spending a ton of time, behind closed doors, with them.

Plus, the beautiful Sam Vash. Our new queen and princess. So smart and poised and vulnerable, all at the same time. If I liked girls, I'd certainly fall in love with her.

I'd see them together quite a bit. Talking, sitting in one of the small study rooms, next to each other on a couch. And several times, I saw them walking on the streets of Fall Creek, near the school. Talking, their heads kind of close together, and one time when they were walking, Sam was holding Levon by the arm. There is just no way you would have seen something like that a year ago, or five or ten years ago. Levon didn't touch people. People didn't touch Levon.

I was pretty sure something was going on between them, but I had absolutely no confirmation from anyone. Anna, who was pretty tight with Sam, swore it was nothing, and you'd think she'd be the first to know.

But the biggest thing for me happened one afternoon, late in the day, after school was over, and I was doing stuff in the library. I came out into the hall, and Levon was walking toward me.

In this flirty, jokey way, I said, Hey, gorgeous.

He stopped in front of me. Then he hugged me. This huge hug, where he actually lifted me off my feet, and said, Oh, Avery. Our Avery.

Then set me gently down.

He was at least five inches taller than me and about ten times as strong, and I remember thinking, If only.

Then we each walked on, and I thought, That is not the same Levon Grady I've known for a dozen years.

And I was dying, just dying, to know what in the name of heaven was going on.

Twenty-nine

~~~~~~~~

Levon

The cold kept on and on and on. We'd have a day or two when it would get warm, and just when you thought it had to break, when you thought it had to get into the twenties or, impossibly, into the thirties, it stayed down in the single digits, or maybe in the low double digits. Eleven, twelve, sometimes even fourteen or fifteen. And at night, always near or below zero. And these absurd windchill factors.

I stayed home and thought about my parents. I did my meetings with Meg and Sam, exchanged a few emails with Trevor, because that's what we decided I should call him.

I wasn't sure what was going on with Sam and me. She spent the night, we had a lovely night, one of the loveliest nights of my life, and then the morning after Christmas, she had to go back home.

I didn't know what it meant exactly. I thought about what Trevor had said about light and love. Maybe I loved Sam.

I certainly cared very deeply for her. She moved me. And I thought she felt the same way about me. We had coffee together, and a few times we went for walks, but mostly I did what I always did, which was go to school and stay home, only it was made worse by this terrible tension between me and Susan. I spoke to her now, but the dynamic had changed. She no longer had a power over me, and I didn't really want to be around her. I kept to my room.

Sometimes I had lunch with Sam, along with Anna, and Avery and Noah and Sierra, and various other seniors. Even though it was still only late February then, we were starting to feel the end of things. All these years together, and soon, bang: all over. Even Sam, who'd only been here six months, was getting that. Anticipatory nostalgia.

With Trevor, we had settled into this once-a-week-or-so email routine. Back and forth. We had decided not to talk on the phone yet, not for a while, maybe not till summer. And we had decided that we wouldn't meet—and we definitely wanted to meet—until late in the year. Maybe at Thanksgiving or Christmas. He said I was taking in so much, and there was the project, and graduation, and Cornell. He didn't want to upset the applecart. We had scads and scads of time.

I liked some of his expressions.

By March, we had a few days in the upper teens and twenties, and I went to Sam's almost by accident, and her mom and dad were both there, and it was a really cool house, almost like a large, really large English cottage off Cayuga Heights Road. She had to pick up a notebook because she'd left some writing she had to show me in it. She pulled into the driveway, and said come in, and I remember thinking, I've never met multimillionaires.

Come say hello, she said.

I think it was Thursday, and the cars were not fancy, though there was an Austin Mini that was bright red, and inside the house was very cool. Spacious, and very tasteful, but comfortable and lived-in, and her dad was wearing two wool sweaters, and said, Hello, Levon, and smiled and shook my hand, and then he said, They weren't kidding about these Ithaca winters, were they?

I said, This is way worse than usual. I mean, even for here.

He said, Come in, and waved me toward the living room, and this graceful woman rose, and she reminded me a little of Susan, though not so intense, and she said, Levon? Am I right?

Glad to meet you, I said, and was thinking to myself, My, but you sound normal, don't you?

She said, This is a terrible thing to do, but my word, you're a handsome, hunky boy, and we've heard so much about you.

Oh, Mom, for God's sake, Sam said. Do you have to embarrass both of us? Are you that clueless?

And her dad said, He seems to be holding up well.

I asked how they were liking Ithaca, and Nathan—he said to call him Nathan—said they really liked Ithaca, and Vera said Ithaca was terrific. She said, Forgive the phrase, but Ithaca is gorges.

It was as though I was acting like a normal person, or practicing to act like a normal person, and doing it, but watching myself at the same time. Thinking, from outside myself, Look at Levon. He seems perfectly normal, with a pretty good set of social skills.

Meeting Sam's parents made me think about Susan. I had been writing about her, of course, and sharing it with Meg and Sam but no one else. Seeing Sam with her parents made me understand her in a whole new way. And I thought it would be interesting to show Sam Susan.

Finally I asked her if she wanted to bite the bullet, and come meet Susan, and she said, Sure, more quickly than I thought she would, given everything I'd been writing about her lately. Susan, at that time, still didn't know about all my emails with Trevor, as far as I knew.

I brought Sam home after school in early March, I think the second week, and it had actually reached the low thirties that day. We walked over from school at lunch, which was maybe four or five blocks, and Sam had her hair in these beautiful blond braids, and she wore a kind of loose blue beret, and when we got inside the front door I called, Susan, and she said, Yes, from the back of the first floor.

We walked through the long hallway and living room, to the kitchen, a short hallway and bathroom, then a dining room that was all unpainted wood and windows, and because Sam was with me I was suddenly seeing it with new eyes. It was very sparse and almost Danish. It looked onto the backyard, which was all trees, and an unpainted gray barn.

Susan stood up from the table, and it was very strange. She was wearing slippers, and I said, This is Sam, and Susan smiled, and they shook hands, and Susan said, Susan, and it was one of the oddest moments of my life. My mother did not seem to know quite what to do. It was like Susan was unmoored, something I'd never seen, but Susan had not been quite the same Susan ever since Christmas.

Sam said, It's nice to meet you. I've heard so much about you, and Susan said, Yes. Thank you. You're doing this secret project with Levon.

Very hush-hush, I said.

Meg, Sam said, has sworn us to secrecy. Said the project could not happen without absolute confidentiality.

So I understand, Susan said.

Sam was wearing boots, and she was nearly as tall as

my mother. And it seemed suddenly, with Sam in the room, that my mother was not nearly so formidable.

Would you like some coffee? Tea? Susan finally said.

Thank you, no, Sam said.

We backed into the kitchen.

Yogurt? Fruit? I asked.

Of course, Sam said.

Sam seemed to be rallying.

This is your first year in Ithaca? Susan said.

Yes.

You must love our salubrious winters.

Sam laughed. I've gotta say, she said, it's been a very impressive winter.

They're not always this bad, Susan said. And you're from Boston?

Yes. My dad worked for Fidelity Investments, in IT security, then he worked for the Harvard Corporation. Then I fell apart, and he now works for Cornell, mostly for institutional investing, for IT security, and he teaches a little at the Johnson School. He's very interested in NGOs.

Nathan Vash? Susan asked. I was reading about him. New faculty. Very interesting. Walked away from the fast track.

I kind of forced his hand a little.

Really?

Mom, I said.

We sat down at the table with yogurt and apples and cheese and tea.

And you're in neurobiology? Sam said.

Yes, Susan said. The human brain. The holy grail. And I know less, I fear, than I did twenty years ago.

Or you know what you don't know, Sam said, which is more than you knew twenty years ago.

Susan laughed.

That's one way of putting it, and I suppose that's true. We know what we don't know, and that puts us a little ahead of where we were.

We were sitting at the table in the back room. Sam and I were eating fruit and yogurt, and I was drinking tea. Susan got up to pour herself more coffee, and when she came back, she sat down across from Sam.

If you don't mind my asking, Susan said, you said you kind of forced your dad's hand, your mother and dad's hand, I presume. What did you mean by that?

Sam swallowed, and I could see her hesitate. They had sent me off to boarding school, she said, where I did not want to be at all—it was really my grandparents' decision—and in the first week, I made a pretty serious suicide attempt. I tried to leave the world. I kind of felt as though I was dying anyway.

Sam unbuckled the strap of her watch, and laid the inside of her left wrist—facing up—on the table. There was a white scar, about an inch and a half long, slightly jagged in the middle, with white dots on each side where the stitches had gone in and out. Even though I knew about that night, I had never seen the scar before.

Oh, child, my mother whispered, and she did something I never would have expected. She picked Sam's wrist up in her hand, and gently and slowly, ran her thumb over the scar.

Poor baby, she said, I'm so terribly sorry.

There were tears in her eyes.

You were how old? Susan asked.

Sixteen.

I'm so sorry, Susan said.

She laid Sam's wrist back down on the table.

Forgive me, Susan said. I don't know what—

Oh, no, please, Sam said. You're a mom. You have a kid the same age. It's—it's just when you feel trapped, you're cornered and you're not thinking.

Sam rebuckled her watch.

Now it's this thing I cover with time. Like. Time heals. Time passes, she said.

So you didn't stay at Groton?

God, no. She laughed. I spent from September to December at McLean, and then January to May at Austen Riggs, in the Berkshires. That was my academic year. Shock treatment to begin with, and then by the end of the year I was getting tutored by Smith and Mount Holyoke students. Reading *The Magic Mountain* and *The Varieties of Religious Experience* and *The Portrait of a Lady*. It was kind of a spring of the James brothers, not far from the Mount, where Henry James visited Edith Wharton. About a mile from where Melville wrote *Moby-Dick*. Enchanted hills.

That's some year, Susan said.

I had been silent this whole time because I was dumbfounded. Believe it or not, it looked as though Susan was a little enchanted with Sam Vash.

And this program with Meg, Susan said, it sounds very mysterious, very top secret, for-eyes-only, as the movies used to say.

They both laughed.

You got me there, Professor, Sam said.

Susan, please.

We're just not supposed to say, right, Levon?

I shook my head.

Meg would have our heads and our souls, I said.

We had to get back to school, and as we left, Susan did something else that was unusual. She asked Sam to come back and have dinner with us, and she leaned over and hugged her. Not a perfunctory hug, but a long, hard hug. A hold-you-to-the-earth hug.

Walking back to school, Sam said, That wasn't anything like what I'd expected.

Me either.

What happened?

I hardly know. But I think she fell a little in love with you. You moved her. You touched her heart.

She was so kind, Sam said.

She's capable of kindness, I guess. And it made me feel the irony, of how Sam immediately elicited Susan's empathy. Maybe Sam's frankness just threw her.

Then it occurred to me, maybe for the first time in my life, that maybe Susan was lonely, that behind the immense confidence there was some small part of her that was a small child, crouched in a corner, more than a little bit scared. It was strange to even think of her that way, but maybe that happened as you got older. Your parents were not omnipotent. They might even deserve our compassion sometimes. It was something I needed to give more thought.

When we got back to school, Avery and Sierra and Anna were at the butt-smoking bench. Somehow, the clouds had broken, at least momentarily, and the sun was shining, pushing the temps up close to thirty, maybe even higher. We sat down, and Avery immediately started in.

Two, three weeks till college letter day, he said. All the colleges said they reported by April 15, but in fact, most of them mailed their application decisions by late March, or very early April. The end is near, he said, then he quickly turned to Sam and me. Which meant it was time to come clean, were we or weren't we? He needed to be the first to know, were we an item? Lovers? Nearly lovers?

And you, he turned to Anna. You, my dear, and she smiled, and sipped from a bottle of green tea. She looked at Sam, and Sam looked at her, and just for a second, I thought I saw something. A flicker, a shadow of a reflection of a smile.

Avery, love, Anna said. You'll always, ever, cross my weaving heart, be the very first. And as for you, handsome, she said to me, how's every little thing? Are you in love yet?

I didn't even blush. I took a sip of my drink, and looked at the sky that almost threatened spring.

Thirty

~~~~~~

Ron

The school year resumed two days after New Year's Day, on a Wednesday, which meant, of course, that it would be a very short week. The kids seemed both tired and excited, and outside it was bitterly, bitterly cold. During the night before, the radio had said we had reached a low of minus seven, and the high that day was supposed to be four degrees. This was the second winter in a row where the temperatures were unusually low, even for Ithaca.

Somehow, I had thought that because a year ago it had been such a harsh winter we would get off easier this year, but it was not looking to be that way, and as it turned out, that second winter would be even more severe.

A friend of mine often joked that she had started to take the weather personally.

But being back among the students was always energizing, and always, always interesting.

I had been doing this work as a school psychologist for more than forty years, and by rights, I suppose, I should have retired, should have given way to younger blood. Taken up fishing or watercolors. But Holly, my wife, was dead ten years then, and what was I to do? Sit home and wither?

And I found the students at the Clock School more challenging, more interesting, more involving to work with than any I had worked with in my long, long career. I felt too that the students liked and felt comfortable with me. As though I was a nonjudgmental grandfather. Too old to get angry, and old enough to have seen and heard most everything. I thought, vaguely, that I'd give it until I was seventy.

I didn't try to be hip or with-it. That would have been comical. I wore my cardigans and corduroy jackets, my khakis, and loafers, my V-neck sweaters, and my door was always open.

Late on the first morning back, Meg stopped by my office and slumped onto the couch. She asked if she could close the door, and I said, Of course.

She said, Ron, I don't get it.

Get what?

These kids.

Do any of us get these kids?

I think of Levon. I think I've known him his entire time

here, and I swear, he's either on drugs, or off drugs, but something strange is going on with him.

How so?

He's just not himself.

I didn't say anything. Silence is often the psychologist's, and teacher's, greatest tool.

You know how with Levon, no matter what, there's a sense that there's a veil, a layer of fabric or glass or fog or something, between him and the rest of the world? Like he's always at least one tick of the dial removed from everything? Well, it's gone. It's really gone.

Have you asked him about it?

Haven't had the chance.

Maybe it's a good thing.

Maybe it's dangerous, she said. He was seen eating lunch with three or four other kids, and he apparently was out at the butt bench drinking coffee after lunch with three or four other kids. In this weather.

Curious.

That has never happened in five and a half years.

I was silent.

Ron, she said. Work with me.

I smiled.

Maybe it's a good thing.

Jesus, she said, and got up, and hurried out.

God, but I liked that woman.

Then one thing struck me, and for a moment I was worried. Schizophrenia often comes on very suddenly to patients in very late adolescence, often around eighteen or twenty years old. And it can seem to happen nearly overnight.

I wondered if that was what worried Meg.

After classes had ended, and most of the students had left, something almost equally curious occurred. I was at work at my desk, it was getting dark outside my window, and there was a soft knock on my door.

I looked up, and it was Levon Grady.

Ron, he said, do you have a few minutes?

Absolutely.

He came in, set his bag and coat on the floor, and sat on the sagging couch.

Over the years I'd seen him perhaps a half dozen or a dozen times, just for routine check-ins.

Can I ask you something? Something very important?

I was almost afraid he was going to ask me if I heard voices too.

Of course you can.

I waited.

I know this will sound weird, he said, and my anxiety rose. Voices? Secret powers?

Do you think I have Asperger's? Am I anywhere on the spectrum?

I think I must have sighed with relief.

Why do you ask?

Can I close the door?

I nodded, and he did.

Because all my life I've had the feeling that I do. I've had that impression. I've read about it, and without saying so, I think that Susan, my mom, gave me the impression that I did.

Funny you should ask. It's all over your school records and evaluations, even though I'm not supposed to tell you that.

That I have Asperger's?

That you don't.

What?

You remember Carrie Miller at Fall Creek?

Yeah. I adored her.

She was convinced you did not, and she was convinced your mother, without saying so, thought you did, or was afraid you did. Carrie pushed your mother hard to have you tested, but Susan absolutely, adamantly refused.

Why?

I think you'd have to ask her.

Do you think I do?

I think you're an exceptionally bright, sensitive kid. You were brought up by an unusually protective mother who seems to have been afraid of something. In retrospect, and everything's easy in retrospect, she didn't need to be afraid. Did this do harm? Let's say it imposed limits that were unnecessary.

So I'm more or less normal?

Levon, what's normal? You're a very bright kid. There's a great British poet, Philip Larkin, who wrote in this poem, "They fuck you up, your mum and dad. / They may not mean to, but they do." It's dark and cynical, and not entirely true, but there's a lot to that, I said.

Levon started laughing. Philip Larkin, he said. "They fuck you up, your mum and dad." God, that's good.

I smiled too.

One other thing, he said.

I looked at him.

I found my dad. We emailed. He's a big physicist at Case Western Reserve University in Cleveland. He knew no more about me than I knew about him, even though he wanted to. It was Susan.

I was surprised. Like everyone else, I'd had no idea.

But he was in a better position than you to find out, I said.

Levon looked thoughtful. I suppose so.

We sat there awhile in silence. The room grew darker and darker. Without my noticing it, the streetlights had come on.

Don't hate Susan, I said as shadows crept across the

room. Don't demonize her. Whatever she did, I think she was trying desperately to protect and love you. She may have fucked you up, as Larkin says, but all parents, in some way, do that to their kids. They may not mean to, but they do.

It was quiet again.

Finally Levon said, Hey, Ron.

I looked at him.

Did you fuck your kids up?

He was putting on his coat, picking up his bag.

We never had kids, I said.

Hmmm, he said. Then, Thanks, and he went out and down the darkening hall.

Thirty-one

~~~~~~

Vera

I remember it, of course, very clearly. Sitting in the great room in the house in Chestnut Hill, watching *Sense and Sensibility* with Alan Rickman and Emma Thompson and Hugh Grant, sipping wine, and Nathan was in his small office just off the big room, doing something on his computer, and my cell phone rang.

This was somewhere around eleven on a Saturday night, and I could see it was from the dean of students at Groton, and I froze for a moment, could feel the panic in my bowels because you don't get good news at that hour from the school where your child is a student.

I answered on the fourth or fifth ring, and a male voice asked if this was Ms. Van Resse, and when I said it was, he identified himself, and said he had some alarming news. That Samantha had harmed herself, had been drinking alcohol alone in her room, had locked herself in the bathroom, had cut her wrist, and had been taken to Emerson Hospital in Concord. The cut was not minor, he said, and I said, Please hold, and called, Nathan. Please, Nathan, louder, the panic in my voice, and he came in, and I handed him the phone.

I heard him say, Yes, this is Nathan Vash, and I sat down on the couch, and took a deep swallow of wine, and heard him say, When? and, Emerson Hospital? And, Do you have an address? And, I'm sure you did all you could. And, Thank you.

He put the phone on the table and said, Let's go. We were both wearing jeans, and I pulled a light coat on, and loafers, and Nathan and I were in the Accord, and he had on a suit jacket and sneakers and we drove to Emerson Hospital, through mostly empty streets, and the emergency room was busy, I seem to remember, and we identified ourselves, and were led to the cubicle where she was lying on a gurney.

Her hair was matted and damp, and she was woozy, and she was very pale. Her left wrist was elevated, and she was surrounded by two nurses and several doctors, and there was an IV line in the back of her right hand, and a monitor for pulse and blood pressure on her upper right arm, and a small clamp on the forefinger of her right hand, and her left wrist was wrapped and elevated.

I wanted to touch her, but the best I could do was stroke

her calf, over the thin hospital blanket, and she didn't seem to see us.

One of the doctors, wearing blue scrubs, with the blue hairnet, took us aside and said that he was Dr. Kimble, that Samantha had cut her wrist, had had a good deal to drink, had lost quite a bit of blood, and was *shocky*, the word he used.

The cut was deep, but luckily had not severed any arteries, but had she not been found when she was, she might have been dead within another hour.

They were waiting for a plastic surgeon who lived in Lexington, who was on the staff at Brigham and Women's in Boston, but who had privileges here at Emerson Hospital, and was coming over to help reattach the severed tendons. He should arrive any minute. Then he would close the wound.

Samantha should spend the night, and he recommended we find a psychiatric facility.

Nathan said, McLean.

The doctor said, McLean would be excellent.

I don't know when I had begun crying. In the car, in the cubicle, in the hallway. But tears were just streaming down my face.

We sat in a waiting room, and sometime later, when someone on the staff found out that Nathan was a vice president of the Harvard Corporation, they put us in a lounge with a bed, and a kitchenette, and comfortable chairs. Nathan sent emails to friends at Harvard, and arranged a bed at McLean, and we spent the night, sleepless, and I don't need to say it, but it was the worst night of my life.

Dr. Pearlman came in around two or three, and said that all had gone well, that Samantha was comfortable, that her wrist would be fine, and that he expected her hand would function normally. He said he was very sorry. He had teenagers of his own. He knew how unpredictable and unexpected and mysterious they could be.

He said he understood that Nathan had arranged for Samantha to be transferred to McLean, that Nathan was on the board of the Harvard Corporation, and he gave Nathan his card and said to call him if there was anything he could do. He said we could see her. That she was in room 217 on the second floor, and he wished us good night. We thanked him.

We sat up all night and held her hand, which was heavily bandaged, and stroked her hair and face, and I said, It's me, Nathan. I did this to her.

No, sweetheart. It's all of us. It's a giant clusterfuck.

We whispered back and forth, over our sleeping child's body.

I said, We need to leave Boston, Chestnut Hill, Groton,

the Van Resses, the all of it. The money, the Benzes, the everything.

He looked thoughtful.

I felt like I wanted to die sometimes, and I guess that feeling never completely goes away.

We had both known we had to change this life, I know now, for a long, long time.

This was the worst night of my life, and of Nathan's life, and probably of Sam's life as well. But from here, from now, from well over a year later, it was one of best moments of our lives too.

It made us see what we had come to. We had somewhere between twenty-five and fifty million dollars. We lived in a museum. But we had no meaning, no purpose, in our lives. We hated ourselves, and what we had become.

After Sam was in McLean, and they said it would be a long stay, perhaps as long as a year, Nathan began to listen to the offers from the headhunters who had always been calling him. Finally, in November, we visited Ithaca and Cornell. We had always heard what a lovely city it was. Nathan would do his usual IT security work, but he could also have a hand in institutional investing, he could teach a little at the Johnson School, their B-School, and I could teach an undergraduate class or two if I wished.

The money was fine—nothing like Fidelity or Harvard,

but it was more than handsome. And we'd never need money again.

We found a lovely house, a house that felt like a home, and moved just after Christmas. McLean recommended that Sam spend the full academic year in a hospital, so she was transferred to Austen Riggs, in Stockbridge, in the Berkshires, roughly halfway between Boston and Ithaca.

This isn't to say it was easy. I found a new shrink in Boston, and then in Ithaca. I took antidepressants. I didn't teach that first spring term in Ithaca, but unlike when Sam had been at McLean, Nathan and I were allowed to make the drive to Stockbridge once a month to see Sam. She was still shaky, but she was calm. She was emerging. She was looking forward to coming home to Ithaca in June.

I took a three-week training course, and began to volunteer at Hospicare. It's a small facility, with six beds, but also services people who choose to spend their last days at home. I work each Sunday night at the main facility, serving meals to those who are still eating, helping to clean up in the kitchen, talking to the patients who want company. Though most do not. Maybe it's my penance for being a disgusting rich bitch for so long.

In their last days, the dying patients begin to draw themselves inward, to somehow prepare themselves on their own terms.

But even when I am only washing pots and pans, loading the dishwasher, cleaning the counters, taking the compost out, past the beautiful gardens, I find the work incredibly rewarding.

Not that I'll ever atone for my sins, or heal Sam's scar or emotional wounds. I'll live with those forever. Just as I know, rationally, that I didn't create Sam's depression, that I suffer from the same disease, the same chemical imbalance, that I'll struggle and do my best, still, deep down, in my heart and bones, I know too that I inflicted scars, and that knowledge will never go away.

Our life now is far from perfect, and I still wonder if Nathan and I, if Sam, will make it okay.

In the fall, I taught my first undergraduate course, Introduction to Business. I was assigned a graduate student to assist me, thank God, because without Becky, I would have been sunk. But it went okay. In the spring term, I was on my own, and I did okay.

I think of Sam, and I watch her, and sometimes I think we are even, in some way, slowly, tentatively, growing less distant. And yet I know, and will never recover from the fact, that it was her life, her blood, that saved us from spiritual hell.

Who was it—some poet—who said that the child is father to the man? He meant it, no doubt, in some deeper, more metaphorical way, but here it is kind of true in a more fundamental way.

So now I watch. I wait. I am careful. I try very, very hard to follow the Hippocratic oath: Do no harm. Because God knows, Nathan knows, Sam knows, I know, I damn near killed my lovely child.

And she, in turn, gave us life. Perhaps without knowing it, she gave us this second chance.

Thirty-two

~~~~~~~

Nathan

The thing I remember best about all those years working and making money, and Sam growing up, is how little I remember. It's all just Teflon and numbers, and dots on a screen. Millions of dots making millions of numbers and the years go by at warp speed. She's a little squirt, then she's lying on a gurney at Emerson Hospital and Vera and I are looking at each other like we're viewing a corpse, wondering how our daughter, our beautiful sixteen-year-old daughter, got dead all of a sudden.

But it wasn't all of a sudden, of course, and we both knew it, and we both knew how and what had happened and why it happened, and we knew it was all going to have to change, and change right away, if we were going to save our daughter and save our souls if we had any souls left to save.

Because selfish as this is to say, miserable as Sam was, at least she was in shock. She wasn't feeling much at that moment. They'd given her drugs and some medicine for the pain of stitches and depression and anxiety, which wasn't to say it would not be agony for her.

But Vera and I didn't have that. All we had was the knowledge that we had, if not caused this—because depression is a disease of the brain, a lack of serotonin and norepinephrine and dopamine, and was inherited—we had paid far too little attention. We had spent the past sixteen years ignoring our daughter, and working, and hiring nurses and nannies and maids and mothers' helpers, and then we'd sent her off to boarding school. That was our part, and we knew it, and we had to live with it.

Now we had our fortune, and we had nothing else.

The only small consolation I had was that my dad, who was dead three years at the time, wasn't around to see this, because I could not have looked him in the eye. He was probably the sole and only normal thing in Sam's childhood and she adored her Pops, as she called him, as he adored her.

He had retired from the post office in his late fifties when they found an irregularity with his heart, and he was eligible for a full pension anyway. I was making the big, big money by then, and he was proud of that, and I kept offering to buy him a house or condo in Newton or Wellesley or West Roxbury, even, but he would never hear of it.

I've got everything I need right here, he said, and in a way, he did.

So after his retirement, he read, listened to music, actually went to the symphony and museums, to Fenway for Sox games, and saw a few old pals from the post office.

Sam loved going to Roslindale. She loved the small houses, the chain-link fences, the Madonna on the half shells in front yards, the mom-and-pop stores and sub shops on corners, the whole small crowded life there.

At the Van Resses' she had to dress up, and be careful not to bump into things, and eat carefully while sitting up straight, and answer carefully and in turn. None of that applied at Pops's house.

Sam loved to climb in his lap, and he loved to cover her eyes and do animal noises and make her guess what animal he was. She could crawl under and around and behind furniture, and sometimes we went to Red Sox games at Fenway. Fidelity had Valet seats, which were high above the action, but Dad got me to trade them for seats a few rows behind the Sox dugout. Sam loved the noise, the rhythm, the vendors, Hey, Coke heah, Hey, hot dogs, Hey, peanuts, and how the vendors tossed the bags of peanuts way down the row to the buyer, and money was passed quickly back and forth from buyer to vendor, hand to hand.

The lights, the Green Monster, Big Papi, Pedroia, and the

giant Citgo sign in Kenmore Square, beyond the outfield, which changed constantly, and as the game got later into the night, the colors of the sky changed, and Sam sat small and warm between me and Pops.

Sometimes, in the middle of an afternoon game, we'd walk down to Sal's, a sub shop, and Sam always got the small meatball sub with provolone, and Sal, the owner, threw in a few bags of chips for Sam 'cause she won the cutest customer of the day contest.

Sam always blushed.

The thing that bothered me, and I guess maybe it shouldn't have bothered me, is that Vera always insisted that I go to these awful dinners at the Van Resses', accompanied by Sam in girly clothes, while I never expected—nor wanted—Vera to come to Roslindale. I think Vera actually liked my dad, but she hated baseball, and where could you shop in Roslindale?

But somehow, I was supposed to pay homage to Jack and Vivian. They were too polite not to ask about my father, but they were not polite enough to invite him to their summer place in Maine, or for a small family gathering in the Back Bay.

And the funny thing was that he probably knew more about music and books, about Kafka and Isaac Babel, about Joyce and Proust, Scarlatti, Bach, and Telemann than they did. He was, in his way, more cultured. He didn't know a sailboat from a hole in the ground, a Cartier watch from a Rolex, but he understood beauty and art and nuance.

The incident that did it for me, though—I guess it was two things—was when my father died, late in August, three years ago, of a massive heart attack. He was home watching the Red Sox, and I took some comfort from that fact.

Sam was very upset, and we had a service at a funeral home in Roslindale. Cremation, followed by a funeral Mass a few days later. My mother- and father-in-law were in the last few days of their summer vacation, and they would not cut it short to attend the funeral. Vera spoke sharply on the phone to them. She said Sam was very upset, but they said blithely that she'd get over it.

But my former professor Ira Rosen, bless him, came to the Mass, and whispered to me afterward, So, your in-laws can't show the respect due to a Catholic/Jew, whose half-Irish son could now buy and sell them.

I'm in a selling mood, I whispered, and he winked.

Then the whole Groton thing. That was the second thing.

Sam had been good at the small, virtually unknown place called the Crafts School. She'd had, I seem to remember, nearly a full year there that was good and happy. And then Jack and Vivian started in on Groton. Groton this and Groton that. FDR and TR, and that, of course, was the Roosevelts. And the heads of the CIA, and the State Department, and every distinguished family since Columbus had landed. And Jack himself had had simply a marvelous time there, and so too had his brother, and his uncle or father or perhaps both.

A real home-like feeling. And a sense of duty, and honor.

What the fuck did I care if Sam felt a sense of duty and honor? I wasn't sending her to fight the Crusades or the heathen Turks at Gallipoli, or the Krauts at the Somme, or even the Commies at Khe Sanh.

How could I have caved on this one? What was I thinking? But by then of course I was at Harvard, and they all thought the world of Groton too.

And Sam. Was she consulted? Even once?

Sam liked the Crafts School.

The Crafts School, Vivian said. The Crafts School.

She herself had gone to Miss Porter's.

So Sam went to Groton. And I thought afterward, Your family. Who is your family? Who loves you? Who looks out for you? And who do you look out for?

And when do you realize you love the people you really love, and that to do that you have to tell those others, the seemers, the pretenders, to back off? To go away?

Thirty-three

~~~~~~~

Sam

I don't know when it started, and I don't know why, but I should have been aware, and I should have been paying attention. This had been happening pretty much all my life, and I'd been told over and over to watch for the signs.

Just pay attention, stupid.

But so much was going on. Levon and all the stuff with his mother and father, and the idea of college, and not having that many more months at the Clock School, where I thought I had finally found a home. Plus writing like crazy, and reading a ton, and not getting enough sleep. And while I was supposed to be taking a maximum of one and a half milligrams of lorazepam a day, I was taking double that dose, to deal with the stress, and to try to get more sleep.

But I'd get in bed exhausted, and my mind would race and obsess, and I'd go over every little thing that happened or was said that day—such as Sierra telling me she loved my coat (was she being ironic?) to something Meg asked, Are you getting all that's here? Are you really digging at this, exhausting it?

Then I just felt exhausted, and gloomy, and then I didn't want to get out of bed. Anna asked if I was okay, and Meg and Levon both said, Is something going on? You doing all right?

I kind of blew them off, and said I thought I was getting a cold, was just really tired, but on Friday I left school early, and when I got home, nobody was home, and I said to myself, That figures.

I went upstairs, got undressed, got into my sweats, and pulled the covers nearly over my head. And that's when I really started to feel it. Like, It's back. Like the whole fucking show. Here we go again.

Just when you thought you were free and well, just when you'd been trying so hard, and working your ass off, the fucking black dog of depression comes sneaking in. Or maybe it was more like a heavy, dense blanket. Just covering you and everything, and the whole fucking world. People everywhere were talking and laughing and smelling flowers and watching movies and reading books, and they were all a billion miles away.

I pulled a pillow over my head, and went into a deep sleep, and Mom woke me around five, and said, Sweetie, you okay?

I said I was tired, and just wanted to sleep.

She sat on the edge of the bed, and felt my forehead, and said, You don't feel feverish.

Can I bring you anything? she asked.

I wanted to say, A gun, but God forbid where that would lead.

No thanks, I just want to sleep some more.

Okay. I'll check in in a while. Dad'll be home soon. Maybe we can order takeout or something.

Sure, I said.

Then I was asleep again, and I don't think I dreamed anything. I was deep, deep down and going deeper, and I could feel myself as though I was a piece of shit, maybe in some half sleep, and completely worthless and useless, and there was nothing to be done about it. No hope. No help. Nothing and nothing and more black nothing.

Somewhere around seven both Mom and Dad came in, and they put the bedside lamp on. Dad sat closer to me and he said, Honey, what's going on here?

Nothing's going on here.

You're feeling bad? he said.

I nodded.

How bad?

Pretty bad.

Like, not physically.

No.

Like what?

I looked at him, then looked at the watch on my wrist.

Like I want to die.

Like you want to die?

Like I feel so awful I wish I could die.

He lifted me in his arms and held me. Mom was stroking my hand.

Sweetheart, Dad said, we have to take you to the ER.

No fucking way.

It's just to check you out.

And spend another year . . .

It's just to check you out. Maybe adjust your meds.
We're getting this before we reach the Groton level, Mom
said.

I got out of bed, and Mom found shoes for me. We got
coats, and while Dad drove, Mom and I sat in the backseat,
her arm around me.

Dad said, I'll call Dr. Felter's office when we get there.

Felter was my meds shrink, a woman in her forties with
enormous brown eyes, who was shy and seemed very
kind. I saw her like every three months for a meds check.

At the hospital they put the plastic wristband around
my wrist, and while Dad dealt with the insurance cards and
paperwork out front, they led me and Mom to one of those
cubicles. It was apparently not very busy for an early Friday
night.

A nurse came in and said, Hi, my name is Staci, and I'll be looking after you.

She took my vitals, and then said, What seems to be the problem?

I feel awful.

Awful how?

Just really, really depressed.

Mom was standing next to me while I lay on the gurney, holding my hand.

Do you feel like killing yourself?

No, absolutely not, I said.

I knew that was the crucial question.

Have you ever attempted suicide?

I didn't say anything.

Have you?

I nodded.

How long ago?

About a year and a half ago.

But you have no plans, no ideas of doing it again?

None whatsoever.

Mom said, She said she wished she were dead.

I just can't stand feeling this way, I said.

A doctor, midforties, fit, compact, came in.

Dr. Kamp, this is Sam Vash, who is extremely depressed, and has a history of suicide attempts.

Attempt. One attempt.

Dad came in and said, Nathan Vash, and shook both the doctor's and nurse's hands. Then he came to me and put his hand on my shoulder. He leaned down and kissed my hair.

It was a pretty serious attempt, and she spent most of last year in McLean and Austen Riggs. She's been doing very well since then, Dad said.

What meds is she on? the doctor asked.

Lithium and lorazepam, I said.

Do you want to kill yourself? Dr. Kamp asked.

No. No. No. Not at all.

Why did you say you wanted to die?

Because I feel beyond awful, and I thought I was done with this depression shit.

Unfortunately, it's a lifelong thing. Luckily, we can manage it, Kamp said.

Have you called Dr. Felter? Kamp asked my dad.

Yes. I got her service, but she's supposed to call back.

And, Staci, you called upstairs?

Yeah. Wendy will be right down.

Kamp took my hand and he looked me in the eye. Listen, kiddo, he said, I have a fourteen-year-old with depression. Dr. Felter's his doctor, in fact. It's tough, but it can be managed very effectively. We'll have you up, dancing, sooner than you think.

Trust me, he said. Wendy, the MSW from Behavioral

Sciences, is coming down to talk to you. We may want to keep you a day or two.

No. No fucking way. I spent a fucking year.

One day, two at most, Kamp said. I promise.

After I talked to Wendy, who was short and chunky, they said I should say goodbye to Mom and Dad. Dr. Felter would be in to see me at ten the next morning. We hugged, and Dad said, I promise, it won't be more than a few days.

They wheeled me down shiny corridors, went left down more shiny corridors, then onto an elevator, and up a level or two. Then through a heavy steel door, into a kind of big corridor with other steel doors, and we went left through one into the adolescent unit.

It was the usual psych ward, only much newer. There seemed to be only five or six patients. But by then it was almost eleven. A couple of kids were in this lounge watching a movie on TV with the sound turned low, and a few more were in their rooms, one reading, two looking at their computers.

A nurse said she had some meds for me, and that I must be very tired. She told me again Dr. Felter would be in early, so that would be good.

I went to the med station at the nurses' pod, and the nurse said, I have two new ones, and lower doses on two others. Venlafaxine is an antidepressant, zaleplon is a sleeping pill, and Dr. Felter wants you to take only half your dose of lithium and one half a lorazepam.

She put the pills in a tiny cup, and poured me water from a pitcher. I swallowed them, then she gave me a toothbrush, soap, and towel, and showed me to my bedroom.

I fell into bed, exhausted and weirdly relieved, and was asleep in under three minutes.

The nurse had to shake me awake at nine, and she even brought me orange juice and a bagel to my room while I was showering. I didn't have a change of clothes, but it wasn't like I'd been out there jogging or anything.

Then they brought me to an office, and there was Dr. Felter, shy, with her amazing brown eyes, wearing jeans, and cool hiking boots, and this beautiful silk scarf.

She actually stood and hugged me, and said, I see the black dog has made a visit, and I explained about the last few weeks, and school, and Levon, and not sleeping, and taking too many lorazepam, and just stressing over everything.

Her eyes were huge and drinking me in, and she said the lorazepam could be having a depressive effect.

And what about this wanting to die? she asked.

I just felt so hopeless and didn't want to go through that whole Groton/McLean/Austen Riggs thing again. I thought I'd been doing so well.

You have been doing so well. You just weren't paying enough attention. You don't want to kill yourself?

Absolutely not.

Here's what I think, she said. The lithium is not working. You need a straight-out antidepressant, so I've started you on venlafaxine. I'm also giving you Sonata to sleep. Take it twenty minutes before you go to bed. It's quick-acting, so don't try to drive on it. Stick to one half milligram of lorazepam, three times a day. With the lithium, wean yourself by taking a half tablet a day for a week, then a half tablet every other day for a week, then off. I'll write all this down.

You following me? she asked.

I nodded.

The other thing is that I want to see you, in my office, once a week, for at least the next month. Can you do that?

Where's your office?

Same block as Gimme!—North Cayuga Street. Downtown. In a big white house. First floor. Can you do Monday at four o'clock?

Yeah. That's right near school.

She took out a card, which had the address, wrote the date, and on the back of the card, she wrote a phone number.

This is my cell phone number. Anything comes up between seven a.m. and ten p.m. you call me. If it's the middle of the night, talk to your mom and dad, and if you have to, come to the ER.

She handed me the card.

Thank you. Thank you for coming in on a Saturday.

You're worth it, sweet girl, she said.

I almost started crying. She took my hand.

We're gonna get through this, she said, and those brown eyes, everything about her, made me believe her.

Okay, I'll write your discharge instructions, some scripts, and have them call Mom and Dad to pick you up.

She hugged me again, then went out.

While I was waiting, sitting in a chair by a window that had this huge view of the lake and hills, I felt almost hopeful. It wasn't as though the heaviness was gone, but I was really, truly leaving after one night. There were new meds to try. And everyone had noticed and listened to me. Mom and Dad, Staci, Dr. Kamp, Wendy, Dr. Felter. I had said what I felt, and they had listened to what I had actually said, and heard me. Like I had asked for help, and every one of them had helped me. It was strange, but looking at the lake, and the beautiful city at the southern end of the lake, I felt something like warmth flooding through me.

Thirty-four

Levon

Sam sent me a text Sunday afternoon, and it was as short and cryptic and as shocking as any message I'd ever gotten from her.

She wrote: Got real depressed. Was in hospital briefly. Am fine now.

I wrote back, Hunh?

She texted, Should I call you?

I wrote back, I'll call you.

She answered on the first ring, and as soon as she said hello, I said, Sam, what's going on? What do you mean you got depressed and were in the hospital?

She said it was kind of a long story, but kind of a short story too.

I said, I need to see you. Now. Can I come over there? Now?

Yeah. Now.

Okay. But please don't be mad, she said.

I'll be there in ten minutes.

And then, before hanging up, I said, Are you okay? Really?

Yes. I'm really okay.

I won't be mad, I said. How could I be mad?

I borrowed Susan's car, and it was weird, because driving up the hill to her house, I was kind of mad. How the hell could this have happened? How could I not have noticed or known? Had she tried to cut herself or kill herself?

I started thinking of the last few weeks, and I couldn't really think of anything that stood out, that had seemed different or depressed about her. Or maybe I was so wrapped up in my own shit, my own narcissistic self, that I just didn't notice. I felt guilty and terrible and confused and really worried.

Sam had been depressed, bad enough to have to go to the hospital, and she hadn't said a word to me. I was whistling past the fucking graveyard, as it were.

I pulled in the driveway, and knocked at the back door, and her dad answered, and he seemed kind of normal. How could he be normal after such a thing?

He said hello and thanked me for coming over, and then Vera came into the kitchen, and she hugged me, and said things were okay.

She said, We've had a little scare, but it's okay. Things will be fine.

Nathan said Sam was in the living room, and they'd leave us to ourselves, and Vera asked if I wanted coffee or water or anything.

I said, No thanks.

Sam was standing in the alcove, near the bay window in the living room, and she looked like Sam. Except, and maybe it was just me, she looked thinner and paler than usual.

I went over and hugged her hard, and hugged her for a long time, and I kept saying, Sam, Sam, and, Oh God, Sam.

She said, Levon, it's okay.

We sat down next to each other on one of the small couches that looked out onto the front lawn. I took her hand and held it, and she said, You don't hate me?

Hate you? How could I hate you? For getting depressed?

For being such a fuck-up, and letting things get to that point, where everything came crashing down.

What happened? Why didn't I notice? Why didn't you tell me? I hate myself for not knowing, for not noticing.

I'm a good actress, she said.

So what happened?

It was gradual and also so sudden, that I didn't even notice, and that was really stupid of me. I mean, I should know. I should be the one paying attention. This is a life-long thing, and I've gotta be aware.

But how—?

I think I was really tired, and stressed and overworked, and just not sleeping very much. Then Friday afternoon—Friday was two days ago and school, right?—I was walking to my car and this heavy gray blanket came over me. Or maybe it was earlier in the day. I can't really remember.

So what'd you do?

I came home and got in bed and pulled the covers over my head. And I just felt like dying.

Holy shit.

Yeah. Holy shit. That's how it feels.

She told me how her mom had come home and how she'd told her she felt terrible, and then when her dad came home she told them she felt like dying and they took her to the ER.

And how kind everybody had been, and how she'd spent the night, and her amazing psychiatrist, Dr. Felter, came in to the psych ward Saturday morning and changed her meds up, and how now she was going to see Dr. Felter every week for a month or two.

Sam had been terrified the whole time that they were going to send her back to McLean or Austen Riggs, but they promised, her mom and dad, the ER doctor, all of them, that she'd only spend one or two nights on the ward. That she'd be home in a day or two. And they kept their word.

So you're feeling pretty okay now? I asked.

Yeah. Pretty decent for a crazy girl.

We sat and looked out the window and held hands. And after a long time she said, Are we okay? Sam and Levon?

We—yes. I stammered for a moment at her use of "Sam and Levon." We're better than okay. You've just got to promise to tell me things. To tell me everything. To let me know if you're stressed or lonely or tired, or if you feel like something's coming on.

Can you promise me that? I asked.

She smiled.

She said, You know what's pretty ironic?

What?

Hearing that coming from you.

How so?

I mean, Mr. Communication. Mr. Transparency. The guy who spends the night with me on Christmas and then shuts me out for three months.

It's just that, if you didn't tell your parents. Damn. I don't even want to think about it.

What's happening to us, Levon? Suddenly she was serious.

I looked out the window, and at first I think I was frowning and perplexed. Then I started to smile, and I said, Meg happened to us, and you happened to me, and all the rest of it is a big mystery, a paradox. Maybe in twenty years I'll understand.

Maybe never, she said.

Then she leaned over, and right there in her parents' living room, she kissed me on the lips.

In broad daylight. As if there were no such thing as secrets.

Thirty-five

~~~~~~

Avery

Well, we knew of at least one grateful young man at the Clock School on April 1, when I went on the New York University website to find that yours truly had been accepted, and that I was, in fact, moving to the southern end of the island of Manhattan in late August. I was in a quiet room at school, and I started whooping it up, and people started pouring in—Meg, Ron, Noah, Sierra, Anna, a bunch of the computer kids, Sam, and finally Levon, and he hugged me so hard, and lifted me, I swear, halfway to the ceiling, though he needn't have.

I was already there.

The colleges had been reporting in dribs and drabs since December with the early-decision applications. Levon and Sam were Cornell, Anna was going to Oberlin, Noah to Williams or Kenyon, a bunch of the computer kids were RIT, Carnegie Mellon, Case Western, and one, surprisingly, to

Williams, which was a fantastic school, but I would have thought somewhere more techie.

I went out so Sierra could have a smoke, and it was actually pushing into the midfifties—jean jacket weather. I asked if she minded all this and she said not really, but she had to admit that she was a little surprised that she did mind a little bit. Like here we all had these definite exciting futures, at definite exciting places, and she had no idea what she was gonna do or where she was gonna be. For all she knew she was gonna be a barista at Starbucks or Gimme! Or maybe working on some organic farm just out of town, like shoveling goat shit, or cleaning out the pens of pigs. That, she bet, could be pretty nasty.

Yeah, but so too could be being stuck at the absolute worst college, in the worst town in the world, with an absolute asshole of a roommate, and parents who said, We paid for this year; you're staying.

That would definitely suck, she said, and she was pretty sure she'd apply in the fall.

So, Sierra, I said, two things.

Yes, my dear.

Two things.

Yes.

Will you visit your first love in the big city, so I can show you all the smoky dens of iniquity at three a.m.?

I absolutely will.

I count on that.

You've got it.

And Levon and Sam? What gives?

I can't help you with that one, she said. Something is definitely going on there. I don't think they're lovers. Not yet. But I think they're heading that way. And some serious shit has happened with Levon.

Why do you say they're not lovers?

Not quite easy enough physically yet. A little too stiff, a little unnatural, almost skittish, but it's coming, no pun intended. I think they're seriously in deep like, if not in love. And Levon's different. I don't know how. It's like he was on a lot of diazepam or sipping martinis between classes. Something's still weighing on him, but he's easier too. Maybe all that father shit. Maybe Sam said or did something. Maybe Susan, though I doubt that. Susan's the immovable object.

I tended to agree with that. Then Sierra went inside.

I was staying outside when Anna came out. She said, You ready for the big city, Avery? And I said, The question, my dear, is: is the big city ready for me?

Now where exactly is Oberlin? I asked, though I knew full well where it was.

Oberlin, Ohio.

And Ohio is where?

Avery, she said, gimme a break.

I offered her my water bottle.

She took it and sipped.

And it's near what municipality?

Does that mean city?

Correct.

Cleveland.

Ah, yes. Cleveland, Ohio. That's on one of the Great Lakes, I believe. Lake Erie?

Anna sucked in more water. And where's NYU? she asked.

Very amusing.

I'm very happy for you.

Me too. For you.

Avery? I have an odd question for you, and I'm only asking because we're coming to the end of school and everything.

Yes? I'm all ears. You have me most intrigued.

Do you think we should ever have tried to go to bed together? Just once? For the hell of it?

She caught me completely off guard. I was oddly touched.

Me and you? In bed together? Naked?

She nodded, and kept nodding.

I don't know. I never considered the idea, though I always thought, just as I always told you, that you were immensely attractive, and pretty much the coolest person in the school. I don't know why it never occurred to me. Did it occur to you?

Sort of?

Any particular reason?

Not really. Just that we're all leaving.

You know something, sweetheart, I said, and I put my hand on the side of her face. I wouldn't rule it in, and I wouldn't rule it out. We have about a month and a half left. And then most of the summer.

And then breaks when we're in college.

We sat in silence for a minute or two.

Does this have anything to do with Levon and Sam?

Why would you think that?

'Cause you're their best friend, and I can't imagine you asking such a question before becoming so tight with them.

Avery, I'm 99 percent positive they're not having sex.

You'd tell me if you knew?

I think that would be up to them. But you'd know.

We sat a little more.

Anna, can I say something?

But of course.

I'm moved and honored to be even considered, in your thoughts, as a possible sexual partner.

Avery, she said, you're a gentleman to the roots of your hair.

I nodded.

And where'd you say you were going to college? she said. Then we were laughing.

Gotcha, she said.

You're going where?

Cleveland, Anna said. It's in Iowa. Near the Great Salt Lake. Lots of Mormons. Great nightlife.

Thirty-six

～～～

Kendall

I arrived at Austen Riggs in January, and my family's from Los Angeles, and it was not just that I was as depressed as I was, but I felt almost as though I was being sent away to the land of the wicked Queen of the North. Not that it wasn't very, very beautiful in its way—the mountains, and the trees, and the amazing whiteness and all of it so clean, and the air so clear and the granite in the bare places in the mountains so gray and hard and solid and very, very old, like it had survived everything, had been there forever, and would be there a whole lot longer.

But the main house was white and huge and so elegant in a way you never saw in LA, just understated, and the great oaks and beeches looked hundreds of years old, and everybody was so quiet and formal and friendly and kind.

And most of all Sam, who I met the first night, when they drove me up from New York City, which was everything

Austen Riggs was not. Loud, crazy, busy, frantic, flashing at you a thousand miles an hour, and I just closed my eyes, and hoped the driver knew where he was going. Which of course he did.

Then north, across, I guess, the George Washington Bridge, then along the Hudson, or near the Hudson, and along highways, and turns, and bit by bit, there were fewer cars, and I saw a sign that we were in Massachusetts. And I knew that Stockbridge was not far across the Massachusetts border.

Then we were on the grounds, and though it was dark, and it was night, the big house was lit up, they received me, and I was given a thorough medical exam, and I was sixteen and very sad and scared, and this girl, a bit older than me, leaned in the doorway after the exam, and said, Hi, Kendall, I'm Sam, I've been appointed kind of as your big sister these first few weeks, so maybe sometime tomorrow I can show you around a little.

I nodded, and stared, because she was beautiful beyond measure, and I had been alone on planes all day, and was very tired, and really low and frightened. And I was half afraid I had come to an awful, punishing place, but here was this graceful, elegant girl, not much older than me.

Try to relax, and get some rest. You must be exhausted. I know that's like saying, Don't think of polar bears, she said, and we both laughed. But you're in a good place.

She stepped in, patted my shoulder, and left.

There are some things, or people, that occur at certain moments, when you exactly need them in just that way in life—and Sam was that for me.

Like there's a line in the Bible, and I'm not even religious, but it says, For I was in prison, and You visited me.

That just gets to me every time. It almost makes me cry. Because I felt like I'd been sent to a kind of prison, a very cushy prison, to be sure, but a prison nonetheless, and Sam was the first person who visited me.

And she was as good as her word, because at breakfast the next morning, she sat down next to me with her tray, and there was a fire going in the fireplace, and she said, I bet this feels like a long way from LA, indicating the snow on the trees and hills outside, and I said, Thousands of miles.

She asked how I'd slept, and I said, Not too well, and she said maybe I was overexcited.

She said that after breakfast, if I didn't have any appointments, or any particular place to be, and if I felt like it, she'd show me around, and I said, Sure, that would be great.

And pretty much from that morning, it was as though I had a big sister, somebody I could always turn to. Someone who had been through a lot, but who never complained, and who always said, Well, that's a tough thing you're going through, that's really, really hard, but you're tougher than you think, and you'll get through it. I know you will.

She was there at the beginning, and she was there until she left in June.

I never came out and told her. I guess I'm still pretty shy, and pretty careful with my emotions, but if I could tell her one thing, it's that I kind of feel she saved me in some small way. Because on a winter night, in a faraway and snowy place, she was the person who visited my prison, and it almost makes tears come to my eyes to think about it, even all this time later. And she was always there. Just quiet and steady and strong.

That's how I think of Sam Vash.

Thirty-seven

~~~~~~~~

Levon

Things had not been great with me and Susan since Christmas. Now it was April, and though we talked and ate dinner together, and said the usual things in passing, there was a certain chill to everything. She seemed somehow not so big, not so confident, and it was as though I had kind of beat up on her, and really hurt her, and I didn't feel so great about that.

Then one night, I think it was a Tuesday or Wednesday, and fairly late because she was in her pajamas and bathrobe and most of the lights on the first floor were off, I stopped her in the doorway to the living room and said, Mom.

This had gone on too long, and I was really beginning to feel for her. And I was beginning to understand that maybe, like me, she didn't have such great people skills.

I opened my arms and hugged her, and because she was

barefoot and I was in my Docs with the inch-and-a-half heel, I felt enormous.

We weren't big huggers or touchers in my family. It went with the territory of Kansas, I guess. You knew you all loved each other. You didn't have to go around showing it all the time.

But I held on tight, towering over her, and I said, Susan, I want you to know that I love you very, very much. And I'm proud of you, and I think you've been a great mom.

Levon, she said in a choked voice, and then she put her arms around me, and clung to me like I was Jesus or Buddha. Oh, honey, I'm so, so sorry. I fucked up bad.

No. You were brave, and adamant, and you loved me.

I could feel her tears on my chest.

I had never witnessed her crying.

Sweetheart, I was young and arrogant and foolish. I thought I knew everything.

I took her hand and led her into the dark living room. We sat on the couch, our sides touching, and I held on to her hand.

You had an unusual kid. I'm not a junkie or in an asylum. I'm not in jail.

But it could have been so much better for you.

On the whole, it was pretty good. I do like to be alone.

But you should have had friends.

I'm making friends this year. Slowly, maybe a little

awkwardly, but I have friends. This thing with Meg and Sam has really made me look at myself and at other people. At empathy. And being vulnerable. I have a long, long way to go. But you know how there're all these social archetypes? The absentminded professor, the whore with a heart of gold, the screwed-up teenager? I'm getting more like the basic screwed-up teenager.

But it's so much more than that, Levon.

But it could have been so much worse. What if you married some nutcase, and I had a crazy father? Say one of your colleagues from your department—Bates or Stoneham?

She started laughing. Bates would have had us all on macrobiotic diets, and you'd still be wetting the bed, and probably sucking your thumb, she said.

And Stoneham would have had you raise me in some Skinner's box, eating raw meat, and going to weekend retreats in sweat lodges where I would've died of heatstroke.

We laughed and then we were silent awhile.

I don't know, honey. I feel so many conflicting things, she said.

I do too. I feel like one of those multiple personalities. Who's gonna wake up today? Angry Billy, Shy Bobby, Aggressive Susie. But a lot of the time I feel almost elated. Like things are changing, and I'm so, so excited by what's happening. The world's getting bigger. It's a little scary, but really cool too.

Then I paused.

But I feel unambiguous love for you.

She looked at me, and her eyes were wet.

And one other thing. And this feels really weird to tell you.

What? she asked.

It feels very strange.

Tell me.

I maybe . . . Then I paused. I might possibly, sort of, be finding, may even have, a girlfriend.

Honestly?

Yeah. I think. We like each other a ton.

Sam?

Yes.

Then we were quiet some more. We were leaning against each other.

Finally I said, Mom, Susan, it's gonna be okay. Nothing's gonna be easy, but I swear, over time, it's gonna be okay. It's just changing. And kind of abruptly and fast. But we'll deal.

You know I love you ferociously, she said.

And as your dad might say, I said, though it's redundant and unnecessary to say so, the feeling is fully mutual.

Then we sat in the dark, in silence, like two old boxers who, exhausted after a long fight, hug in the middle of the ring after battering each other for twelve rounds, who feel a certain respect and admiration and maybe even a kind of love for each other, because only they know what they have just gone through.

Thirty-eight

~~~~~~~~

Sam

Life had been good lately, I had to say. The new meds seemed to be working, and seeing Dr. Felter had been kind of cool. She had this wonderful office, with this lovely maroon carpet, a couch, and these deep chairs, and a few bookcases, and this real abstract art on the walls.

Every shrink's office I've ever seen had abstract art on the walls. No landscapes, no portraits, no still lifes. I guess they wanted you to free-associate or something, or not to be able to make too much of a recognizable object. That would be too un-Freudian.

But no African masks, though every other shrink's office I'd seen had at least one African mask, or an African basket or something, as though that was supposed to bring us back to our earliest primitive roots. Didn't the human race all start out in Africa? Didn't Freud love African art?

The light was muted, and I just felt really safe and comfortable there, the way I felt in Meg's office.

And stuff with Levon and school, with Mom and Dad, was cool. I was afraid they were gonna hover over me after the hospital, check my emotional blood pressure and pulse twice a day, but they really treated me—not as if nothing had happened—but as if something had happened but that we had dealt with it, and we were all gonna be more mindful and alert and vigilant, I guess you'd call it.

It made me think quite a bit of two years ago, and being in that shower, and what if I had talked to someone instead of drinking vodka and grabbing an X-Acto knife. I had felt at the time that I had nobody to talk to, and in a weird way, that I had no voice. No way of articulating what was inside me to anyone in the outside world. To anyone outside my own trapped thoughts and my own trapped head.

By then it was spring in Ithaca, and as everyone had always been saying, spring in Ithaca was a glory. Just our yard alone. It went crazy with flowers and trees and bushes and buds, and on warm days, my parents, me and Levon, me and Anna, we'd sit outside, and sip tea, or just sit, and the colors, the layers of lawn and rock terraces—lavender and yellow, and red and orange and blue, and I swear, there was almost nothing that was simply green. I mean, the grass was green, and the big trees had these pale green buds, but everything was color and light, and all the colors changed in the sunlight, depending on the time of day.

It was like that horticulture professor had really been an artist, not a scientist, and his eye was perfect and everything was grace and harmony.

We were almost finished with senior year, and our project was nearly done, and it was all hard to believe. That I had friends. That I loved Levon so much, and I was pretty sure he loved me back just as much. And I had Anna and Avery. I had Noah, and even Sierra. And my mom and dad were becoming almost normal regular people. They went out together, and they laughed and talked with each other, and for parents, that was almost a miracle.

I mean, they were still parents. They still drove me a little crazy, but they were really okay. They were doing the best they could.

And I thought a lot about Meg Goldman, and what an amazing teacher, what an amazing woman she was. She was tough and tender, and she saw everything. She pushed us when we needed to be pushed, and hugged us when we needed to be hugged. And I kept thinking, How on earth did she know to pair me off with Levon for the project?

I mean, she didn't even know me. And knowing Levon now, it could have gone way wrong. Looking back, I was pretty shaky at the beginning of the year, and he was Levon the withdrawn. How did she know that writing about our history and our daily lives would have such an effect on us?

Did she know we'd fall in love? She couldn't have. We might just as easily have ended up fighting like cats in a bag. Or just curling up and withdrawing to our separate corners.

But she knew. And my Lord, look what's happened.

Now I guess it's all coming to a close. Senior year at the Clock School. And that kind of scares me and excites me, and does all kinds of things to me.

Plus, I really don't want to get too happy and confident and up. That's a little dangerous for me, because I'll always crash afterward. I've got to be really careful and mindful and aware and vigilant. I've got to watch out all the time for signs of the black dog. Because he's always there, somewhere, waiting.

He's very, very patient. I've got to stay in my skin. I've got to be still, but still move forward, and that's way harder than you'd think.

But I can talk now. I have friends and parents. More than anything, I have a voice.

And I didn't have that before.

Thirty-nine

~~~~~~~

Susan

He showed me the email he wrote to Trevor back in January, I guess it was. He wrote the email in January.

That evolution in students, their changing so much during the semesters, happens every school year. The winter is longer and tougher than you ever think it will be, despite the snowdrops and crocuses, and you somehow think that winter has killed all the plants and flowers and trees. But spring does come. You see the thickening buds, you see green sprouts, and by mid- to late April, there we are again, and by May you wonder how you ever doubted it in the first place.

I was hurt and a little shocked by Levon's first email to Trevor, though there was nothing he said that was untrue. Just that I was unaware, and surprised and even shocked by how unaware I was. And I was even more shocked by Trevor's response, because I had been, in fact, completely in the dark about his background, his poverty, his extreme shyness and sense of social displacement. I was not aware that the life of tenant farmers was still going on in remote parts of rural England as late as the 1980s, and that Trevor had spent his first six or seven years as the child of share-croppers, with no indoor plumbing, and extreme working conditions, and what a profound effect that would have on his personality.

I was wrong to have judged him based on such scanty evidence. Terribly wrong and unfair. I was not wrong to be attracted to him, for that I surely was, and to recognize how unique and brilliant he was, but I have been thinking long and deeply and guiltily about this, and I do not like what I see. Was part of the attraction the presumption that he had Asperger's, and I wanted to see if my sexual powers could overcome that, even for one night? Partly true. But I also wanted to give him something of myself, and I wanted to express my deep fondness for him and empathy for his loneliness.

And why the separateness? That, I don't know. The sex was unprotected. I knew that from the start, and I knew going to dinner that night I was going to have sex with Trevor, and that there could be consequences. But part of it was pride. I could raise a child alone.

But there was definitely the Asperger's question with both of them. I assumed there must be an Asperger's link genetically, and when I, when research began to show that it was weaker than I had assumed, there was the behavior or modeling factor. If Levon met or knew his father, if he visited with him, and saw the odd behavior, the one-sided verbosity, the lack of social skills, the lack of give-and-take, he would in a sense have that behavior reified. It would somehow make that behavior more acceptable.

What I failed to see, and feel now, was that like his dad, Levon was shy and bookish, needed some time and encouragement to engage socially, and he would have been fine. But I only ever saw, or feared I saw, Asperger's, and I was determined they would not label my child as such.

And without realizing it, I kind of turned Levon into a young man who resembles in many ways someone with Asperger's. The shyness, the obsessiveness, the lack of social skills—and that might have been why I was terribly moved by Samantha, that lovely young woman who was recently here.

Not just that she was so lovely, but her poise, her style, her courage and frankness, and the absolutely matter-of-fact way with which she talked about her family and her recent history. No self-pity.

I don't think it will be that uncomplicated for Levon and me. Not that it's uncomplicated for Samantha and her parents, but for us, I think maybe the damage will never be undone.

I remember years ago, I was at a weeklong conference at the FBI Academy at Quantico, in Virginia, on the subject of serial killers and violent offenders. I sat on a panel with one of the most famous forensic psychiatrists in the world, a man who had been the principal prosecution witness at the trials of John Hinckley Jr., who shot President Reagan; Arthur Shawcross, who killed children and hookers; and Jeffrey Dahmer, who killed, dismembered, and partially ate seventeen young men in Milwaukee.

There were two or three hundred hardened police detectives in the room, and this man was riveting, especially on the subject of Dahmer. He had spent two or three straight days, six or seven hours a day, interviewing Dahmer in great detail about his crimes.

During Q&A, a detective asked the psychiatrist what he did after spending a long day interviewing Jeffrey Dahmer.

In a flat voice, with no affect, the psychiatrist said, I'd take a long, hot shower, eat dinner, then go to my hotel room, double-lock the door, and lie in bed and read gun magazines.

Gun magazines? I piped up.

The psychiatrist looked at me and nodded.

I wonder what a psychiatrist would make of that? I joked, but the psychiatrist didn't even smile.

I'll never forget that. Because why would he smile? He

had spent twenty-five years dealing with the darkest, ugliest things human beings are capable of, and he was an expert marksman. Why wouldn't he read gun magazines?

My point, I guess, is that we go so far into our own little worlds that we lose our way. All of us.

At one time, in graduate school, and for several years afterward, we thought we had found the Psychopath Gene. In simple terms, we thought that we had found monoamine oxidase A, an enzyme that degrades amine neurotransmitters, such as dopamine, norepinephrine, and serotonin, and we thought that this had much to do with aggression, with the Warrior Gene, and we were finding it in high levels in certain races. Aha. What social implications. Follow this research and we'll have less violence in the world.

But as it played out, and as our research became more sophisticated, we found, using PET scans, that people suffering major clinical depression had MAO-A levels 34 percent higher than average. More like the results you'd expect for people ready to go out to war.

What we did find out wasn't what we had expected, but it did have a profound impact on patients with depression.

All of which brings us around to the fact that we get it wrong.

I got it wrong.

I caused real damage to my son. If I could do it over I would.

But I love him deeply, and he knows that. He has always known that. And I believe he loves me.

He has a different set of data to work with now. Already— the young lady is a case in point—we are seeing different results.

We will move on. There is hope.

Forty

~~~~~

Meg

I find it hard to believe how each year, despite the tears, the panics, the crises, the various impossible and insurmountable obstacles, we arrive at late May again and again and again. The ice and snow are gone. The maple and oak, the beech and ash, the forsythia, the lilac, the tulip and rose, the daisy and jonquil—the thousands of flowers and trees and weeds and grasses—have survived the ice and cold, even twenty-two below, for week after week, even when we were taking the cold personally, when the polar vortex broke records in twenty-seven states, when snowfall levels reached an unheard-of record of ninety-six inches, or one hundred six inches in a half dozen cities.

Spring somehow arrives. And when the drowsy-sounding, busy buzz of bees carrying pollen from flower to flower makes me want to nap on weekend afternoons, it's here. We had four straight days in mid-May when the temperatures hit the mid- to upper eighties, as the colleges began to empty out, and our kids were getting restless, especially our seniors, who were putting the final touches on their various projects.

Then the temps took several steps down the ladders, and by midweek, we had a day when the high was fifty-six, and freeze warnings for overnight, so the big rule, as it always is, is that everything changes all the time, everywhere, all the time.

The whole thing about Sam's brief plunge, the visit to the ER, seems almost like a blip, but a scary reminder too. Sam was back in school by the following Monday, and she said she didn't know what it was, maybe it was some kind of placebo effect, but she had started to feel pretty decent already. Maybe it was about getting more sleep, maybe it was that she'd talked, and she'd asked for help, and every single person listened and every single person helped her. And spending only one night. God, that was so wonderful for her to walk out of the hospital after one brief night.

And then there were tears in her eyes, and she hugged me, right there in my office, and she said, Thanks, Meg. I love you.

To which I could only say, Oh, honey. What did I do?

You taught me to speak.

I couldn't, didn't, say how moved I was.

They hadn't quite finished, but I'd read about 90 percent

of Sam and Levon's project, and I have to say, they'd far exceeded my expectations. In pretty much every way. They had written well over a hundred pages, and at least another hundred or two hundred pages had been written about them, and I don't need to speak to the content. It speaks very clearly and eloquently for itself.

The thing that surprised me, though, was Sam. I'd had some rough idea of what I might possibly get from Levon, if everything went as well as it could go. If each part and piece clicked exactly into just the right place. I'd known Levon a long time, and even knowing him I had as much doubt as hope. But he delivered, and he delivered big.

Sam was the unknown. I had never met her, knew her only on paper, and though there was a great deal about her on paper, I'd never seen her or talked to her. And I must admit I had this small nagging thing about very rich kids, and it's not entirely fair. That some of them lack grit, that there's a tiny measure of entitlement. So I had some sliver of doubt about Sam.

But when I met her, and then as the days and weeks went by, and I watched as she dealt with Levon, and all the swings and gyrations, I not only began to admire her, she kind of became my hero. She never lost her poise, her courage, her grace. She was so consistently strong and on-target that I'd often fail to see just how extraordinary she was.

It's wishful thinking, of course, and it's none of my

business, but I hope they become an item. But that's asking life to become a little too much like a bad movie.

So one more week, and we pretty much wrap things up with the seniors. Then two weeks, and we free the younger ones for the summer too.

Then Ithaca becomes Ithaca for the summer. Shorts and sandals and sailing. Water moving in the gorges, long hikes, dinner and wine on the back decks at the houses of friends. Fireflies, and insects making their insect noises in the dark as we sit and talk and laugh around candlelight. All will seem well with the world. This small part of it, at least.

Forty-one

~~~~~~~~~~

Levon

A few weeks after spring got really under way, Sam said that her parents were going to Boston for the weekend to see her grandparents. They hadn't been there in almost a year, and her dad in particular was not crazy about the idea, and her mom was not much more enthusiastic. But they had to do their duty, and they were letting Sam stay home alone, which was some kind of record in human history, or at least in her family history. A milestone anyway. And she thought that maybe I wanted to come over and hang out, that we could do whatever. Ask some friends over, Avery, Sierra, Noah, Anna, whoever.

Or not.

Whatever, she said.

Did that sound like a teenager? she asked.

I said it did, but that that was fine because she was, in fact, a teenager.

I said I'd check to see if I could get the car from Susan, and Sam said she could just pick me up, but I said it would be fine with Susan. That she thought Sam hung the moon. Susan had a kind of Homeric epithet for Sam; instead of "gray-eyed Athena," it was "that lovely girl."

Stop, Sam said.

So I did, and said I'd see her around seven.

When I asked Susan she didn't so much as blink when she asked if I'd be staying the night. I said I didn't know, and she said if I had even one beer she wanted me to spend the night.

I suddenly felt the urge, and I hugged her, and kissed her on the forehead.

When Sam had told me her house had been owned by a horticulture professor, it was winter, but by then, in late May, it was just a thing to behold. Not that there was this riot of flowers like a funeral parlor, but bushes and trees, flowers, rock walls, and paths, and curves and light, all done in these ways you didn't even notice for a while. And terraces, and stuff that would take days and weeks to even notice, and maybe years. The colors, and the way one shape or color was set near another, and was shaded and shaped near another.

I swear, I'm no garden type, but I could have spent hours out there.

Instead we just sat outside until it was getting dark.

Sam's hair was in two loose braids, and she had a dark top with thin straps, and I could see the black straps of her bra. She wore tan shorts and sandals. I wore my usual Docs and short-sleeved white shirt buttoned to the top and khakis. We sat at the dining room table and had this salad of avocado and tortellini and tomato and pesto, and I'd never tasted half the things that were in it. Plus the wine. It was delicious.

Did you make this? I asked, and she nodded.

Wow! I said.

It's easy.

Right, I said. They always say that.

And the wine's good, I told her. I bet you know the vintage and country and region and everything. Italy, France.

Try New York, homeboy, Sam said.

Really?

Snob, she said.

Okay. You got me. I wouldn't know it from MD 20/20, but it's good.

Tell me, she said.

Yes?

Do you get out much in the summer?

Why do you ask?

I was wondering if that's your summer wardrobe.

I hadn't given it much thought.

We could take you shopping, she said.

That's possible.

Shorts. Sandals. Take you swimming, if you swim.

I'm quite the swimmer, I said.

Oh.

Lessons at the Y.

Ah.

And like learning to ride a bicycle, I began.

You never forget.

Clever.

Shrewd, she said. I was wondering.

Yes?

Since I've seen your boudoir, if you might like to see mine.

Why, how prescient.

I thought so.

I'd be honored, and most curious, I said.

And while it would lack the drama, the unusual timing of my Christmas visit, it would not lack for interest.

We stood up, and she held her glass and the wine bottle in one hand and took my hand with the other.

We went up the steps slowly, and on the second-floor landing, there was a table with a small light burning.

We went up a third flight, on polished oak stairs, and there was moonlight from a half-full moon falling through windows on bare wood. There were three doors, and we went through the one on the left.

The room was long, and had three large windows at the far end, a queen-size bed, a few stuffed animals—a frog, a bear—a comforter, a couch and an easy chair, a desk, and a small coffee table in front of the couch.

Please, sir, have a seat, she said, indicating a place on the end of the couch.

I sat, sipped wine, and she said, So, tell me, please, how long have you been having these problems?

And when I looked up, she had leaned forward, and she had begun to kiss me, lightly, her lips tasting like wine from New York State, only warmer, softer, possibly sweeter.

Forty-two

~~~~~~

Sam

I sat down next to him, and we kissed, slow and light and soft. We sipped wine, and made small sounds, and kept going very slow, but became somehow deeper too.

Then we were no longer sipping wine, and we had begun to use our tongues and hands, the braids in my hair were undone, and he whispered, Soft, and then I was unbuttoning his shirt, and his shoes were off, and then his socks.

I don't know how or when exactly, but we were on the bed, and his shirt was off, and my top and bra were off, and he was licking and kissing, making sounds, saying, God, God, so lovely, so, so lovely.

And it was.

Then the pants and shorts, and we were only skin, just flesh.

I had set out a condom and laid a towel down before,

because this was indeed a first time. But we were still slow. We were entwined, and we kissed.

And everywhere, we touched, and stroked, and his skin was smooth and warm and cool, all at the same time. His body so long, and so beautiful, like I'd known, like heaven, or beyond that too.

And it was beyond imagination, it was my love, my Levon, and he said Sam Sam Sam, oh sweetheart, he said.

And then I shuddered, I thought I would die or fly, and then he shuddered, and we were sweaty, and we were one person, we were together, and we were breathing together— our bones, blood, breath.

Then we were lying on our sides, and he kissed me, and I said, Levon, and he said, Sam, and I asked if he was cold, and he said he was, a little, and I pulled the duvet up, and, underneath, we held hands. And it was very late then. And we were, I was, as happy as I had ever been in my life.

I guess I should end the story there, when everything was kind of just perfect. That was, forgive me, the climax of the story.

But stories go on, time goes on, and stories don't end, even, I guess, when people die. I mean, they have kids who live on, and the things the dead people did in life continue to have some kind of influence on the living, even if it's subtle and unseen.

Meg had given us full-bound copies of our project, with the title, *Sam and Levon*, on the cover.

It was over three hundred pages with all the outside contributions. We leafed through it, and talked about it, and then decided we should wait one year before we read the whole thing. Too much had happened, and things were going too well, and we just thought we should get some distance before we plunged back into the year.

So we finished the semester, and we had this really great summer, hanging out. My first real Ithaca summer, and in some way, Levon's first Ithaca summer, hanging out with friends—with Noah, Anna, Sierra, Avery, and some others.

I got a job at a day-care place up on campus, just twenty hours a week, but it was fun, and Levon worked in a lab in, of all departments, physics, which I found kind of interesting. We all went swimming a bunch, and went to hear live music, and drank beer, and smoked a little weed, and Levon and I were fucking as though we had invented the act, which is to say, almost every night.

It was the best summer of my life, and we all talked about college, and what we were gonna do. We gave Avery a lot of shit about NYU and Manhattan, and Anna about Oberlin, Ohio, but I guess all of us had one eye on college. Noah had surprised a lot of us by deciding on NEC, the New England Conservatory of Music in Boston, to study cello, which was slightly weird, because a lot of us didn't even know he played cello, and NEC was one of the great music schools. Maybe that was one of his disabilities. Intense humility. Which I would call a virtue.

Then in August I did something really dumb with Levon. I don't know if I was worried or testing him or what. I guess I had heard about couples going off to college and kind of playing it loose, saying, Yeah, you can kind of see other people, you can sort of date other people. Not be tied down, start a new phase of life. But maybe it was a test, a stupid dare. We had been together constantly all summer, and maybe part of me wanted to see how he'd react, to see if he really, truly, deeply loved me.

So one night, in bed, I brought up the idea that maybe we should go to school, to Cornell, fresh and unencumbered. Unattached.

You mean split up? he almost shouted.

Not split up exactly. But kind of go with a clean slate. And see what happens. Just a kind of experiment.

Are you serious?

Well, college is a new start.

You don't love me?

Levon, I love you beyond anything.

So for weeks we went around and around.

He thought it was crazy, then he saw the sense of it.

I thought it was sensible, then I thought it was stupid. We cried, we laughed, we raged.

Shouldn't he have said, No fucking way, in the first place? And stuck to that?

But then again, shouldn't I have never come up with the whole moronic idea?

As move-in day approached, we had sort of agreed to try it. We'd talk, have lunch, but we wouldn't be lovers, and we were free to see other people.

Then move-in day came, and it was nuts. Twenty thousand students from around the world, classes, new people, new everything. I was taking two English, a history, and a biology class for nonscience majors, and Levon shocked me when he texted that he was taking two physics, one calculus, and the Course of Justice, kind of a philosophy/political science/English class.

And things were full. I was busy all the time. Classes, a lab, just the effort of meeting people, getting used to the pace, the social scene, the sheer size of life on the hill. I mean, there were something like sixteen libraries.

Levon and I would text and email; we only spoke once on the phone, but neither of us was ever much for the phone. He was always brief. He said he loved physics, and found it strange; one course was called What Is Light?

I went to a few parties. Met lots of people, but nobody who particularly caught my attention. I was kind of amazed that even in a school this big, I had never once run into Levon.

Then in late September, walking across the arts quad, at

the far corner near the architecture buildings, I saw Levon—I could tell even from a distance—near the middle of the quad, walking with an absolutely gorgeous, perfect, half-Asian, half-Anglo girl. She wore boots, and a white scarf and tweed coat, and she was leaning forward and into him at the same time and they were laughing.

The sight went through me like a blade. She was so lovely, and he, of course, was gorgeous, and I thought, So this is what you wanted? This was unencumbered. This was the clean slate.

I couldn't stop thinking about it for days. So much so that I went to a party that weekend, got half-drunk, and started talking to this big, handsome, drunk guy, who was hitting on me hard. I was just a little tempted, thinking of Levon and the beautiful girl, but I blew him off. I think his name was Jason or Mason.

I went back to my room and took a shower, then got in bed, and I felt even more miserable afterward. Just low, and lonely and kind of purposeless. Not the way I felt at Groton, not that level at all. But as normal life goes, pretty low on the shitty scale.

Then one night in October, a Thursday toward the end of the month, I was getting ready to leave Uris, the main undergraduate library on the arts quad. It was after ten, and I'd packed up my junk and was coming down the main interior steps when my phone vibrated.

I pulled it out, and it was a text from Levon, who I hadn't heard from in at least a month.

Hey, he said.

Hey yourself.

Where r u?

Ithaca.

Where on campus?

Why?

Need to c u.

Now?

Yes. Very now.

Why

Can't do this no see shit.

Really?

This sucks. I hate it what were u thinking.

I hate it 2.

Where r u

Uris. U?

Rockefeller

Rockefeller was about three buildings away.

Can u walk toward the rock? Levon wrote.

& u walk toward uris?

Yes

Yes.

I zipped my coat, stepped outside, hoisted my backpack. It was cool, but a lovely fall evening. That clear, clean air, perhaps a quarter waxing moon, and the leaves just about in full turn.

There were not many people out.

I started slowly up the very slight hill, past Olin, then I saw him come out the south door of Rockefeller. A tall young man, with wild curly hair, carrying a courier's bag over one shoulder.

Here we were in moonlight, I thought, two fools, late of a Thursday, desperate to see each other, full of hope like every two fools who had ever loved each other.

And I thought, Here as well as any other place, to end the story that never really ends. Because next week Levon might withdraw and I'll want space. Or I'll get sad and Levon will get hurt. Much as I'd like the story to end in this moment of moonlight, it will go on.

Levon, my love, I thought, and imagined him thinking, Sam, Sam, Sam. Oh Sam. It was awful without you.

And that was why love was like light. Why it was both wave and particle—so slippery and elusive and so terribly hard to keep and hold and even begin to understand.

A mystery and a paradox. But also strange and beautiful. And why we kept trying.

Acknowledgments

My heartfelt thanks to my brilliant editor, Katherine Jacobs, to Elisabeth Weed, Elizabeth H. Clark, Martha Collins, John Lauricella, Ed Hardy, Julie Schumacher, Professor Paul McEuen, George Witte, Madeleine Moss, Dr. Adam Law, Professor Ted Everett, Jennifer Sale, John Vasile, everyone at The Book Group and Roaring Brook Press, and always and especially, to Liz, Liam, and Austin—who move the moon and the stars.